SOME DAY MY PRINCE WILL COME

Natalie Kleinman

SAPERE
BOOKS

SOME DAY MY PRINCE WILL COME

Published by Sapere Books.

24 Trafalgar Road, Ilkley, LS29 8HH,
United Kingdom

saperebooks.com

ISBN: 978-0-85495-067-6

CHAPTER ONE

England 1819

Rebecca Ware pulled the scarf more tightly around her neck and rested the palms of her gloved hands on the wall of the old wishing well, leaning forward slightly, a winsome little smile playing about her lips. She and her older brother, Brew Ware, were at Austerly House, their childhood home in the village of Knapton to the south of the shire.

"I would give much to know your thoughts, Becca," said Brew, standing on the other side and watching her with interest.

Her eyes flashed at her brother and she laughed. "It wouldn't take an exceptional intellect to read what is on my mind. Surely you remember when we stood here years ago as children?"

Brew's face clouded over as the memory returned. Sixteen years before, he, Rebecca and their younger sister Nancy had each made a wish beside the well. Not realising the danger, four-year-old Nancy had later returned to the well by herself and fallen in, tragically losing her life. "It's a time no-one in this family will ever forget," Brew replied quietly. "A tragedy that will remain with us to the end of our days."

"It was," said Becca, faltering as the grief rushed back. She took a moment and then attempted to dispel the gloom. "But this past year has seen great changes for both of us, and the biggest is yet to come. I can't believe you are soon to be a father."

The frown was driven from Brew's face and his smile returned. "So what were you thinking that made you look so mischievous?"

Becca walked around to the other side of the well and tucked her hand in Brew's arm. Both were blessed with thick blond hair, though Rebecca's had been teased neatly into place where her brother's, unfashionably long, fell onto his forehead. Piercing blue eyes lent animation to both and, while Brew's nose was longer and Becca's features softer, there could be no denying the connection.

"I was thinking of my five-year-old self and remembering my wish," said Becca.

"Ah yes. And I have roasted you many times since. Do you still yearn for your prince?"

"Of course I do. I am certain that one day he will come," she replied with a roguish smile. "After all, your wish came true. You became a major and fought at Waterloo. While I am waiting for mine to be fulfilled, I am content and looking forward so much to joining you and Harriet in London for the coming season. She is determined to go, is she not, even though she is increasing rapidly now."

"She is keen to see her mother. We will travel in easy stages."

Rebecca laughed. "Easy stages? Such a manner of progress and Harriet seem not to go together. I shall be happy to accompany her in the carriage if you would prefer to ride," she offered.

They walked back to the house, arm in arm. Becca squeezed Brew's elbow when he thanked her, accepting her offer with no small measure of relief. There was no way, he said, that his wife would be content to travel so sedately while he trotted along beside her. Like him she preferred to ride, but if Rebecca was in the carriage with her she could not complain, and though Becca was an accomplished horsewoman, she was as content to be driven. As well not to tease Harriet when they were well aware that the restriction of her daily rides was, in her own opinion, the only downside to her condition.

Becca could feel her excitement mounting when, only twenty-four hours later, she looked around her bedchamber on the day prior to their departure. She reflected upon what her feelings had been as she had stood there more than a year ago, ready to make the same journey. It had been her first visit to the capital at the age of twenty and, like any other young woman embarking on the social whirl that was the London season, she had been nervous and in high spirits at the same time. Brew and her father, Cornelius Ware, had been estranged back then, and Cornelius had been reluctant to make the trip under circumstances that were an embarrassment to him. He had always lacked the funds to keep Austerly in good repair, and so Rebecca's first season had only been made possible by a bequest from her deceased godmother. It had taken her mother, Elizabeth Ware, almost a full two years to persuade Cornelius to accompany them to London, for he was not an easy man.

Rebecca sighed and contemplated her image in the standing mirror, but her thoughts were of her brother. After being invalided out of the army following the Battle of Waterloo — and having grown weary of his civilian life in Paris, where he had stayed for three years after the battle — Brew had arrived in London just before the rest of his family. After a difficult start, he had managed to reconcile with his father. His talent for cards had made him a very wealthy man, and so he was now financing long overdue improvements at Austerly, as well as sponsoring Becca's second season in London.

How fortunate you returned to England when you did, Brew, she thought now. *My story might have been very different had you stayed away and our family shamed as well as divided.*

Rebecca gave herself a mental shake and prepared to join her parents for supper. It did no good to reflect upon what might so easily have been her ruin. She'd had a lucky escape, for Brew's old friend Gil Carstairs and Harriet had saved her from a disastrous elopement with a man named Dorian Fletcher, who had taken advantage of her youth and inexperience. But for the moment at least, she put the unpleasant memory aside.

Brew had returned to Winthrop, where he and Harriet had been residing since their marriage. They were to collect her the following morning. Elizabeth and Cornelius would remain in Lincolnshire, since her father was no longer sufficiently fit to undertake such a journey. Becca would miss her mother, she knew, but Harriet had become like a sister to her and her own mother, Louisa Lambert, would be in London too. She would be well cared for. Experience had taught her how important these people were in her life. Without them she would have had quite another tale to tell. Well, she was a year older now and not, she hoped, quite so ready to succumb to the charms of a man who had been only too ready to sacrifice her reputation for his own ends. Was Dorian still in France? she wondered. Did he ever think of her as she did of him, or had he found another innocent to take her place? Best not to allow him to occupy her thoughts. The passion she had felt for him had long since died, in its place contempt, but she could not easily forget the intensity of her first love.

She had joked with her brother about finding her 'prince'. Whatever else she may have lacked, she was blessed with a ready sense of humour, but she had to admit to herself that fairy tales were a thing of the past. Dorian Fletcher had robbed her of a little magic, and it had taken her close on twelve months to fully recover her former spirits. Time had given her a new maturity. *And tomorrow I go to London*, she thought, the smile that was never long absent transforming her face as she went down to the dining room.

There was a fair breeze blowing from the east across the flat Lincolnshire landscape, but the sun was shining, and the early morning spring chill gave way to a pleasant day. With no urgency to reach their destination, the party stopped twice before arriving at their lodgings for the night. Brew had done his research well, giving Becca and Harriet the opportunity to stretch their legs without too many hours cramped up inside the carriage.

"We must be grateful the wind has dropped," Becca said as they strolled in the garden of the inn where first they halted. "You might otherwise have been swept off your feet, Harriet."

Her sister-in-law laughed, running a hand over her swollen stomach. "I think between us, this babe and I have enough weight to keep my feet firmly on the ground even in the most ferocious weather."

Becca paused and laid her fingers on Harriet's arm. "You may have been wondering, for we haven't spoken of this matter for many months, if I am apprehensive about returning to town." The look of concern on Harriet's face told her she had judged correctly, though no comment was offered. "One last time you must allow me to thank you for your actions last year, which saved not only my reputation but my sanity too." Harriet started to protest, but Rebecca was determined to have her say. "I would be lying if I said I don't from time to time think about what happened, but my reflections are all positive. I will know in future how to conduct myself without falling prey to such a man as Dorian Fletcher. As long as he remains in France, I can be at ease and enter company without fear. And you know how I love to dance." Becca laughed and twirled around on the spot.

"Well, you must take the floor often with your brother then, for I fear that at present, I can only attend dances as an observer, and you know Brew's leg is much improved. He has become fond of the activity, and he's quite a show-off, given the opportunity."

Brew, who had been settling with the landlord, walked across the grass towards them and was eager to know what it was that they found so amusing. Neither would tell, and he knew better than to press them for an answer, so he escorted them back to the waiting carriage before mounting his horse. Settling back against the cushions once more, Becca asked Harriet, "Do you plan to visit Merivale before your confinement?"

"Yes, in two or three weeks' time, all being well. You are aware, I know, how great is my attachment to my old home. I was so grateful when Brew purchased it for me as a wedding gift. I think my heart might have broken had it passed into the hands of another family. Will you come with us? You may of course remain in town with Mama, if the idea conjures up bad memories for you."

After helping to rescue Becca from Dorian the previous year, Harriet had brought her to Merivale, her childhood home, to recover from the ordeal. They had then put it about that Becca had accompanied Harriet there for a visit, to prevent rumours of the elopement from spreading.

"I have only good memories of Merivale, Harriet, for it was there, thanks to you and Gil Carstairs, that I came to realise I was safe. Will Louisa not wish to go as well?"

"No, my mother never had the fondness for the place that was shared by me and my father before he died. She will much prefer to remain in London and will be happy to escort you to as many functions as you have the opportunity to attend, so do not make your choice in haste. You may later wish to change your mind."

"We shall see," Becca said and both lapsed into silence, enjoying the view to be had out of the windows and content in each other's company.

Neither Becca nor Harriet had stayed at the house in Grosvenor Square before, Harriet because Brew had taken her straight into Lincolnshire after their wedding and Becca because her time in London a year ago had been spent in the property her parents had hired for the season in Duke Street. The Grosvenor Square house was an imposing residence, purchased by Brew the previous year upon his return from Paris, just before he'd met Harriet. In anticipation of their arrival, all had been made ready for a prolonged visit. It did, however, lack a woman's touch. Following a tour of inspection — for Brew was anxious to show them both everything that was at their disposal — Harriet said confidingly when her husband was out of earshot, "All my reliance is upon you, Becca, for you have such excellent taste and will help lighten our surroundings without imposing such vulgar ostentation as would not suit us at all."

Rebecca glanced over to where her brother was talking to one of the footmen. He was immaculate as ever, only his unruly shock of hair giving relief to the black and silver he habitually wore. She adored him, but she understood exactly what her sister-in-law meant. Major Ware was conservative in his style of dress, as with most other things in his life. Harriet, more at home in the country than in town, had no inclination to set a new fashion or to become the rage, and certainly not in her current condition. Everything about her was modest, though with her chestnut hair and green eyes she would always attract admiring attention.

"My brother is not flamboyant, that's for sure," Becca conceded. "But surely, my dearest sister, you have no need of my help when you have such a fine touch yourself. I remember your sister Amabel's ball and how you arranged the garden in such a way as to make it seem an extension of the house."

"It's true that I enjoy such things. At present, though, refurbishing is a task that seems to have assumed huge proportions. Don't tell Brew, for I would not want him to worry, and indeed there is no need, but I am finding myself to be very tired these days. Perfectly natural, I am sure, but you know what men are."

Becca laughed and agreed. Her sister-in-law was an independent young woman who would find it burdensome to be overly pampered. She had for several years been in the habit of running a household. Nothing was more certain than that Brew would be more concerned than the situation warranted if he thought his wife was ailing in any way and Harriet, feeling well enough, would not welcome an excess of attention.

"How you must be wishing to see your mother once more after all this time, Harriet. Does she hire the house in Hay Hill again this year?"

"No, she is to stay with Aunt Matilda. You are aware, each being widowed, that they live for much of the year in perfect harmony in Sawcroft House. Since my uncle and Aunt Matilda never had any children of their own, it seemed advantageous for both to reside together once your brother and I were married. She deemed it unnecessary, therefore, to undertake the expense of a hired property when they might continue the arrangement at my aunt's London residence for the season. St James's Square is more than able to accommodate the two of them."

Becca smiled. She had been a little intimidated by Harriet's Aunt Matilda — Lady Sawcroft, as she was known to respectable society — but she had warmed to her as she'd spent more time in her company. "I remember your aunt so well. A redoubtable lady who likes to give the impression of severity, but who beneath all has a kind heart."

"And it took me years to realise for you must know, when I was a child, she had a preference for Amabel, two years younger than I and by far the more engaging. I ought to have been a boy."

Brew joined them and, hearing Harriet's last comment, he remarked emphatically, "Well, I for one am more than glad you are not. I see you are once more getting your heads together. May I suggest that we retire for a while to recover from our travels and meet again at dinner?"

"Yes, I should be grateful for a period of quiet reflection," said Rebecca, smiling inwardly at her brother's barely concealed concern for his wife and fully understanding that he wished her to lie on her bed for an hour or two. He was such a caring husband.

After retiring to her room, Rebecca stood by the window, gazing out onto the street, she wondered if she would ever find such a man to take care of her. With a little sigh, she turned away and sat at the small escritoire placed against one of the walls. Taking paper and ink, she began to write.

My dearest Mama

We have arrived safely in London and you will be pleased to know we enjoyed a comfortable journey, Brew having had the forethought to arrange all beforehand. I am even now sitting in the prettiest bedchamber, all hung with pink chintz and decorated in a very feminine style. I suspect it was thus when my brother purchased the house, for it is not in his style at all. The rest of the house (he insisted we see all bar the servants' quarters, when we had barely removed our bonnets and pelisses) is somewhat austere, and Harriet begs that I will aid her in giving the rooms some softer touches. She is a little weary after being on the road for two days, but otherwise well and looking forward to seeing Louisa after such a long period without her — a sentiment I fully understand, for you must know that I am missing you already. I trust my father is recovering well from his last setback and that you might be able to join me for a few weeks if he is content to let you go. Certainly the house is large enough to accommodate any number of guests.

My understanding is that Louisa Lambert and Lady Sawcroft will arrive in a day or so and that the latter has already put arrangements in place for a soirée and a visit to the theatre, so you need not fear that we shall be idle. I had forgotten how noisy the streets of London are but am in no way put out. It feels so alive! No doubt I shall be pining for the quiet of the country before too long, but for the moment I am excited above anticipation.

Please give my love to Papa. I shall write again soon.

Ah, I have just recalled that Harriet spoke of going to Merivale for some weeks and invites me to join them. Nothing is yet in place, but if there is any possibility that you can come to London we must ensure that I am here. It is by no means certain in any case that I shall go into Kent with them.

I think that is all for the time being. I send my fondest love.
Becca

One week after arriving in London, Becca felt as though she'd never been away. Once it was known that the Wares were in town, invitations began to flood in. Last year's clothes were outmoded, and new fashions necessitated several shopping trips to supplement or replace what Becca already possessed. In this she was ably assisted by Louisa Lambert, whose impeccable taste guided her when she needed help.

"I cannot tell why it is, Louisa, but though I can usually recognise the style I think will suit, I sometimes find I'm uncertain as to which fabric to choose."

"That is why shopping here is so superior to more provincial areas. There is an abundance of choice, sometimes too much so. I dare say the fascination will never pall, and you will remember from when you were here before how much I enjoy shopping. With Harriet tiring so easily at the moment, it is joy for me to join you as a companion on these trips."

"And a chaperone. I am fully aware of my debt to you. Now, tell me if you will, which of these muslins shall it be? The ivory or the pale blue?"

"With your colouring you can wear almost anything, but I think the ivory with your blonde hair will look admirable, perhaps embellished with some pale orange embroidery or ribbons. On the other hand, why not both?" Louisa asked jokingly.

Becca was acutely aware that it was her brother, not Papa, who was funding her trip. Major changes had taken place at home since Brew had been permitted to throw a sizeable amount of money at the previously neglected property and its adjoining land. Their father's pride had suffered a huge blow, but he had come to terms with the fact that if his son were one day to inherit Austerly, he must be permitted to invest in its future. Becca too had inherited the family dignity and self-respect and would not allow herself to take advantage of her brother's generosity. The blue muslin was rejected. It was a small gesture and one of many she made. It succeeded in making her feel better and the ivory fabric, when made up and decorated as Louisa Lambert had suggested, was everything she'd hoped it would be.

CHAPTER TWO

It didn't take Becca very long to realise that, much as she loved her home in Lincolnshire, town life suited her very well. She enjoyed the company of others, as well as the theatre, the parties and the shopping. She was as comfortable with Louisa Lambert and Lady Sawcroft as with people of her own generation. No longer plagued by the natural shyness of the young and inexperienced, Rebecca Ware, at twenty-one years old, was aware that she had grown up. People she had met the year before were once again in London and friendships were soon renewed.

One afternoon, on returning from a walk in the park with a young woman whose acquaintance she had made at a supper party, Becca found the entrance hall of the Grosvenor Square house not serene and welcoming as usual, but filled with activity. A man's hat, gloves and cloak had been carelessly flung on a side table, and two footmen were in the process of removing luggage placed so precariously in the middle of the floor as to constitute a hazard. Her brother was wringing the hand of a stranger with an enthusiasm that indicated that the man in question was a friend, and welcome. Even as Becca stepped through the front door, she heard her brother say, "Hugo, by all that's marvellous, where have you sprung from, as if I needed to ask?"

It didn't require Brew's pronunciation of the name to inform her that the visitor was French; she could guess as much from his manner. Becoming aware of her presence, the man turned towards her, swept an exaggerated bow and said, "*Charmante*. Mademoiselle, there is no need to tell me who you are. The

17

resemblance is strong, though in a woman so much more *attrayante*. I am at your feet."

Brew laughed aloud and drew his sister forward. "Allow me to present my very good friend, the Comte du Berge. The man is a rogue, Becca. Don't believe a word he says. Hugo, my sister, Rebecca."

"*Enchanté*, Mademoiselle. I have heard much about you. But do my eyes deceive me? Whenever Brew has spoken of you, it has been as of a child."

"I apprehend, sir, that your friendship with my brother stems from his time in France. We have only recently reunited after many years apart. No doubt he thought of me as a child, for so I was when he had last seen me. In fact," she added, indignation her uppermost emotion, "he still treats me as such."

"*Mais non*! A bud which has grown into a beautiful bloom, *n'est ce pas?*"

He was outrageous, but it was impossible not to respond to this charm. She chose to ignore his comment and asked instead, "Am I to understand that you are staying here, Monsieur le Comte? I must assume it was your trunk being carried away."

He threw his arms wide and tried to look apologetic. "You permit? Your brother has been kind enough to invite me to remain."

"Invite you? How so when all was unloaded from your carriage before I even entered the hall?" his host demanded.

Hugo made another unsuccessful attempt at contrition but instead ended by laughing. "I knew, my friend, that you would not turn me away in my hour of need."

"Much you know. Tomorrow I shall pack you off to a hotel, but for tonight you may remain here."

"Mademoiselle Ware, I beg you will use your influence. I have no acquaintance in London. A foreigner in a strange land. Would you allow the major to turn me away?"

"It is not for me to say, sir. Perhaps you should save your pleas for Mrs Ware."

"Your *maman* is here? Brew, how can this be?"

Brew was enjoying himself immensely. With a broad grin, he said, "No, Hugo, not my mother but my wife."

The Frenchman turned in astonishment from Becca to her brother. "You are married!"

"And soon to become a father."

Hugo clapped Brew on the shoulder, and Rebecca slipped quietly away to allow the two men time to renew their friendship. But there was a bubble of laughter inside her as she anticipated that supper that evening would be a far from formal occasion.

Hugo happily followed his friend into the library, full of curiosity and keen to be enlightened.

"How is it that you did not write to inform me of your marriage? Something hasty perhaps, not in the normal way?" He had asked the question in all innocence and was staggered when Brew turned on him with something approaching fire in his eyes.

"You will speak of Harriet with civility, Hugo. Must you always assume there is a vulgar side to everything?"

The comte had never seen his friend ignite in this manner before and retracted immediately. "You misunderstand. I meant no disrespect. I apologise most sincerely." He was rewarded with a relaxation in the other's countenance. "Tell me then, Brew, how did you meet the lady? I am eager to know all."

"You will recall, for you filled my belly with wine the day before I left Paris, that I returned to England little more than a year ago in the hope of bringing about a reconciliation with my sire."

"And you were none too optimistic, thus my motive for plying you with, how you say, the Dutch courage. Did all go well, then?"

"Not at first. So badly, in fact, that I must tell you, Hugo, had it not been for my meeting Harriet, you may well have found me once more in France, my courage gone and my sorrows being drowned."

Hugo crossed one elegantly clad leg across the other and leaned back in his chair. His appearance was in contrast to that of his host, though both were immaculately dressed. Where Brew was fair, Hugo's hair gleamed almost black in the light from the window. His attire, as simple as the other's, was of the palest of hues, his pantaloons being a dove-grey matched exactly to his waistcoat, his coat but a few shades deeper. The only similarity between them was perhaps the silver buttons each sported on his coat.

"You perceive me, I wait to hear all. Tell me from the beginning."

"I will, but not now. Much has happened since last we met, my friend, and the telling of it will take some time. For the moment, suffice it to say that I have found my happiness. For the rest, we will talk about it tomorrow when you have settled in and recovered from your journey."

"I am not such a poor creature," Hugo said, laughing, but he rose as Brew did. "However, if I am to meet the beautiful Harriet and the *chère* Rebecca later today, I must shake off the dust of my journey and change into something more suitable," he added, flicking some imaginary speck from his sleeve.

"No doubt you will stun us all with some new French fashion," Brew said, escorting his friend to the bedchamber that had been allotted to him.

"*Non*, *mon ami*. My taste remains simple. Exquisite but simple. Which reminds me, what of Gil Carstairs, he of the rather more extravagant disposition? He is well?"

Brew laughed out loud. "He is well indeed, my friend, and married also. To my wife's sister, Amabel."

Hugo groaned. "Never say so! You make me feel old. Is there a glass in this room? I must search and see if there is any grey in my hair."

"Should you find any, there is always boot blacking," Brew said and went away, laughing.

Hugo required no boot black, nor did he rush to inspect his image in the glass. His valet was before him but, aside from allowing his footwear to be pulled and his coat to be removed, he dismissed the man with instructions to return in time to help him dress for dinner. Thereafter he laid himself upon the bed, one ankle across the other, arms folded behind his head, and gave himself to contemplation of all he had heard thus far.

Even in the short time he'd spent with Brew downstairs, it was evident he was a changed man. In Paris, where last he'd seen him, he'd been what Hugo would have called a man's man, though he'd had a very pretty ladybird under his protection. But there had been a reserve, a part of him he'd held back, and for reasons which the Frenchman understood implicitly. Both had suffered loss. They'd confided in each other, possibly by reason of recognition of a kindred spirit. Each, for different reasons, blamed themselves for circumstances. Well, it seemed his friend had resolved his problems. Hugo's were outstanding still, and he was beginning to lose hope that there would ever be the outcome he hoped for. That didn't prevent him from trying. For the time being, though, he had run into an impenetrable wall and was taking this time across the water for a little respite and the opportunity to catch up with his friend. Brew hadn't been difficult to trace and, had he not been found to be in London, Hugo would have travelled into Lincolnshire. He was pleased not to have had the necessity, and now he was looking forward to meeting Harriet and reacquainting himself with the beautiful Miss Ware, who was so evidently not the child of his imagination.

Roused from slumber some time later by the faithful Henri, and with the light now faded to black on a moonless night, he stirred himself enough to allow the man to help him dress, his raiment already having been laid out.

"*Zut alors*! Am I a child to have fallen asleep so easily?" groaned Hugo.

The valet merely smiled, suspecting rightly that his master had succumbed to weariness after the relief of finding his friend at home and thus, hopefully, affording him a period of rest after much travelling.

"You are like a cat, my friend, to have crept in, opened drawers and pulled out my clothes, without waking me," Hugo went on, swinging his legs over the side of the bed to sit and run his fingers through his hair. "But it's as well you have come. I would not wish to be late to dine on my first day here."

"There is a lady, I understand, monsieur."

"A very beautiful lady, and the sister of my host. I need not ask how you are aware. No doubt you have gossiped enough already."

Henri look affronted. "I do not gossip, sir. Merely I have renewed my acquaintance with François, the major's man."

"Ah, I recall you were always as thick as thieves. You will be aware, then, that Major Ware is now wed and a child is expected soon. It seems the last year has been good to him," Hugo said with a wistful smile.

"We will come about also, monsieur, I am sure. And, if you do not find what you seek, you will know at least that you did everything you could, *n'est ce pas*?"

An unaccustomed cloud fell across Hugo's face before he clapped his hands together with an assertion that nothing would be solved if he were first to die of hunger. "But you have chosen well, Henri. The cream will suit admirably." With that, he stripped and washed himself at the bowl set on the dresser before turning once more to his companion with a smile. Henri had been with him for many years, and there wasn't much he didn't know about him. He was aware of the sadness, for instance, that was hardly ever seen by others but never far beneath the surface.

Becca dressed with extra care, for she would have been less than human had she not wished to look her best for the handsome Frenchman with whom she was to dine. The ivory muslin, so newly acquired but not yet worn, was enhanced with a sprig of orange silk flowers in her hair, the colour exactly matching the adornments on the dress. As she surveyed herself in the glass, she was satisfied.

There had been no instant recognition that she had met her fate when she'd encountered Hugo earlier that day, only a response to a charming man with a sense of humour. Ready for what she was certain would be an entertaining evening, she tapped on the door of Harriet's bedchamber and was pleased to find her alone.

"Come in, dearest. Brew has gone down before me, as I understand we have a visitor. A friend from his days in Paris."

"Yes, I met him when I returned from my walk this afternoon."

"And? Did you like him?"

"He is very Gallic! He swept me, oh, such a bow. It isn't fair, Harry, that a man may speak the same words with a French accent as an Englishman in his own tongue but that they should sound so entirely different."

They laughed, and Harriet said, "I perceive then that he is a charmer."

"Without a doubt, but you must believe me when I tell you that it is his sense of humour which I found charming, nothing else."

The assertion was not made with any degree of fervour because Becca had spoken only the truth. To say she wouldn't have recognised him again, having seen him for only a few moments, could not have been the truth, but until she entered the drawing room she would have been hard put to describe him. Hugo and Brew were standing on either side of the fireplace, the one in cream and gold, the other in black and silver. Neither was conscious of the picture they presented, but it was Harriet who controlled a little gasp before moving forward to greet her guest.

"Monsieur le Comte, it is a pleasure to meet you. My husband has mentioned you as a friend during his time in France, when things were perhaps not so easy for him. You must allow me to welcome you for that alone."

Harriet was then given an example of the bow her sister-in-law had previously described, after which Hugo straightened up, took her hand and kissed her fingertips.

"You do me honour, Madame Ware. And may I congratulate you on your marriage? Brew is a lucky dog."

"You may indeed, but we do not stand on ceremony with friends here. Please call me Harriet." She turned to glance over her shoulder at Rebecca. "You were quite right. Very Gallic," she remarked and both chuckled.

"You mock me," he grinned, "but it is in the blood. However, I can be as English as the rest of you." He then surprised them by altering his carriage and asking them in a very different manner if they had enjoyed the afternoon and would they permit him to escort them to dinner.

Becca was the first to comment, evidently astonished. "There is no trace of an accent! I wish I could speak your language half as well as you do mine."

"It was not my intention to deceive you, Mademoiselle. I was raised in England from the age of two. Though we spoke French at home, my uncle would reprimand me severely if I did so, or with any kind of intonation, when we were in company. He considered it a mark of respect."

"And now?"

"Now I prefer not to present a misleading face to the world."

Brew, who had been watching the interchange with interest, took his wife's arm and they led the others to the adjacent dining room. He was aware of his friend's circumstances and knew how quickly he could, as it were, change hats. As they sat at the table, Rebecca asked Hugo the obvious question. "Your uncle? You were orphaned?" she said with so much compassion as to touch something deep within him.

All at once, the jovial man became serious. "In truth, I know not. It was at a time of great trouble in my country and many feared for their lives. I grew to adulthood believing my uncle to be my father and only learned of my error upon his death four years ago. It was soon after that I returned to France, where I met your brother some time later."

He paused as food was brought to the table. This was not something to be discussed in front of the servants and Becca, seeing his discomfort, changed the subject with ease, asking if he were to remain long in England.

"I have made no definite plans, Mademoiselle. I came on impulse in the hope of finding my friend, but I own a small property in Hertfordshire and may possibly spend some time there." He waved his hands. "Nothing is yet arranged."

Beneath the table where they could not be seen, Brew grasped Harriet's hand and she said, "I do hope you will come to visit with us at Merivale House. It is my old home in Kent, and we are to go there in a few weeks to await our child."

"I would be *de trop, non?*"

Harriet laughed. "We mean to spend a month or two there. I sincerely trust the birth will not take so long, and there is much to entertain if you like horses and enjoy bleak scenery."

"She is forthright, *votre femme*," Hugo said, raising an eyebrow at Brew.

"My wife says what she thinks, certainly. I have learned not to be embarrassed."

"What? What did I say? Oh, about the baby, you mean. Well, it is natural for me to talk about it. People are in my opinion far too reserved about what is, after all, such a natural occurrence."

"Do not restrain yourself on my account," said Hugo. "It is quite charming."

Becca was moved to remark, "You won't say that when she really gets to know you, Hugo. I may call you Hugo? She remarked only the other day, when we were at the milliner, that the hat I was trying on was quite hideous."

"And was it?"

"Oh yes, Harriet's taste is impeccable. The embarrassment was by cause of the lady standing behind her wearing the exact same creation. I didn't know where to look, I can tell you."

There was much laughter throughout the course of the meal, but Rebecca was keen for it to be over. She was eager to learn more of Hugo and what had happened to his family. Eventually Harriet suggested they leave the men to their port, and they returned to the drawing room.

"Did I not tell you true, Harriet? But I must say, I don't know how I did not laugh when first we joined them. Standing on either side of the fireplace, they looked like nothing more or less than opposing chess pieces."

"Ha, you thought so too? But so handsome, both."

Becca had to agree. "I wonder what it is, the mystery of Hugo's past. There is sadness there, don't you agree?"

"Oh yes. Hugo reminded me of Brew when we first met. On the surface, all is well, but beneath … a tragedy that came from his soul. I felt it too, when I met you."

"Well, none of us will forget Nancy, but it was harder for my brother because he felt the blame was his. And I was but five when she died. Old enough to remember, but of an age when children accept and move on, I think. And thanks to you, Harriet, Brew has to some large degree been able to do the same."

"He is more accepting, I agree. Hugo, on the other hand, has not yet found his redemption. I wonder if he will feel able to confide in us. I did think, in the dining room, that had the servants not been there he would have done so."

"You are right, I'm sure. We must not push him. I think him quite a private man beneath all that French bravado."

"You are sensitive, and I believe you to be correct. We can only give him the opportunity, should he wish to bestow his trust on us."

"Thank you, Thomas, that will be all," Brew said as the port was poured and the bottle left to hand. Hugo had moved to sit close by him and, elbows on the table, was twirling his glass between his fingers. He then looked around the room. It was a comfortable enough apartment, the chairs well-upholstered in the same dark gold silk that adorned the windows. The walls, which were papered in patterned stripes of only a slightly lighter hue, added minimal contrast. It was pleasing enough but lacked a certain touch. No expense had been spared, but neither could there be any doubt it was the work of a man. Harriet had been right in her assertion that the place needed a woman's softness to turn it from a house into a home.

"Well, my friend, who shall go first?" asked Brew as Hugo's eyes came to rest once more upon his friend.

"You, without a doubt. You have obviously had a very busy year." His host laughed and pushed back his chair, flinging one leg carelessly across the other. "For a start, I observe that your injury no longer seems to trouble you."

"And for that I have Sir William Knighton to thank. I consulted him soon after I came to London and he assured me that, would I but stick to the regimen he prescribed, he saw no reason why my limp should not in time be cured, and so it proved to be."

"Then I am filled with joy for you, *mon ami*, for I know how much it irked. It was not such plain sailing with your father, I understand?"

"No, Hugo, that took a little longer, and it was some time before I could believe we might reach a reconciliation. We have our moments still, but for the most part we rub along pretty well together. And I rejoice to see my mother happy after so many years of estrangement."

"You are living with them at Austerly?"

Brew laughed. "No, that would be pushing my luck a little too far, I fear, but Harriet and I live only a short distance away and we see them often."

"She's quite a woman, your Harriet."

"Don't I know it! And fearless when it comes to horses. It is the one thing that irks her in her present condition, that she cannot ride, and I am in no way surprised that she mentioned her cattle when inviting you to Merivale. They are normally with us in Lincolnshire, but she has had them removed to Kent in order to see them each day when we are there. She cannot bear to be parted from them for long. Will you join us, do you think? What are your plans?"

"As for plans, I have none. Only eventually to return to France and continue my search. It has been fruitless so far, and the truth is that it has become such an obsession with me that I needed to remove myself for a while, or I would have gone mad."

"I cannot imagine the turmoil you are suffering. At least I knew my parents were alive when I ran away to join the army."

"I find it hard to forgive my uncle for keeping me in the dark. While I understand the necessity when I was a child, why in heaven's name did he not enlighten me as I grew to adulthood?"

"You must remember he died unexpectedly, or so you told me. And you were still only a young man at the time. Perhaps he was waiting for the right moment."

Hugo looked at his friend, so much sadness was there in his countenance. "Is there ever a right moment? Still I mourn his loss and must at least be grateful that he left such documentation as to tell me where to begin my search."

"The château has revealed nothing so far?"

"It is but a shell, or it was when first I went there. I have begun some restoration work and you may imagine how I have looked, in vain thus far, for any hidden rooms or concealed niches."

They'd spoken of this before, many times. Hugo's château, as Brew understood it, was a large building set in extensive grounds on the banks of the Loire. If it held secrets that were intended to be kept, they would be hard to find.

"Are there many who lived in the area before who still reside nearby? Have you learned nothing from them?"

"Either they don't know or they aren't saying. There is still much fear, even so long after the revolution. But I do not despair, *mon ami*. And in the meantime, it is gracious of you and your wife to accept me so readily. As for Merivale, does the beautiful Rebecca go with you? I fear I must reserve my decision until I know. If she remains in London, then I believe I must also do so. Yes, truly I must."

Both were laughing as they rose from the table and went to join the ladies. Brew could only be glad that Hugo's good humour had returned and the look of despair had gone from his features.

Becca and Harriet were condemned to disappointment, whether by reason of Hugo's not wishing to dwell longer on what pained him or because no-one steered the conversation in that direction. Instead, he asked Harriet about Merivale.

"It is my childhood home, monsieur, set in countryside that can be forbidding, I know, but there is a magic to the place. Mama was never especially fond of it and lives now with her sister-in-law, content to have returned to her roots. My sister, I think Brew told you, is married to Gil Carstairs and resides in Lincolnshire, not far from our own home. When he saw the pain it would give me to part with Merivale, my husband bought it for me as a wedding gift." The look of love she cast at Brew was clear for all to see. "With my confinement drawing close, we decided to come to London, for I had not seen my mother for many months and she chose to meet us here. And then I had this feeling, something I can't explain, that makes me want my child to be born where I was."

Brew took up the story. "So my wife would have it that we write to my old nurse, who lives with us now, and arrange for her to proceed to Merivale and await us there. Whether or not Harriet's mama, Louisa, comes too remains to be seen. She may stay in town, and my sister with her, or she may come to Kent, in which case Rebecca will come too. It is possible also that our own mother will join us, if my father is well enough to let her go. So you see, nothing has yet been decided."

"And you invite me to join this mêlée?" Hugo laughed, vastly amused.

"Well, one thing I can promise you, my friend. You will not be bored."

"Brew, I understood you had left your wild life behind you and settled down at last. I see now how mistaken I was. Whatever it was that made me think you would settle for a quiet life, I cannot imagine. Mrs Ware," Hugo said, turning to Harriet, "I salute you." And he did.

CHAPTER THREE

The next three weeks flew by. A series of social events were attended, and it seemed to Rebecca that she'd barely spent a few hours at home. At every dance her hand was solicited, and she was never seen amongst the ranks of those young ladies who sat on the side while others whirled about the room. At the theatre where her brother kept a box, there were always visitors eager to pay their respects during the intervals. When she walked in the park, so surrounded was she by admiring gentlemen that Lady Sawcroft, taking a drive in her carriage one day, insisted on taking her up. "I must rescue you from such a crowd," she said. "You are doing very well, my dear, by all accounts."

"By my accounts, she means," said Louisa Lambert, who had been Becca's companion on her walk.

"Well, I don't need you to inform me that this young lady has become the new toast of the town. I have eyes in my head, you know."

Becca loved these exchanges between the two women, both such strong personalities. There might have been the potential for some interesting clashes, but there was so much affection there that none occurred — not that she had ever seen, anyway. Harriet, she knew, was pleased things had worked out so well for her mother. The only thing that detracted from her own happiness was the fact that after a few days in Grosvenor Square, Hugo had removed himself to Hertfordshire just when she'd become used to having him around.

"I am desolated to leave you all," he had told all three Wares, "but you will recall I mentioned having a house a little way north of London. I feel obliged to go there, just for a week or two. The matter of a few papers to look at, you understand, and I would wish to be back in time to join you in Kent."

Becca strove to conceal her disappointment. There was no doubt that she was strongly attracted to the Frenchman. It was not love, an emotion she thought she'd experienced some months ago and from which she had fortunately recovered. No, it was more of a meeting of minds. An affection. She felt at ease with him. All this she told herself, but a little of her sense of contentment went away when he was gone, though even her sister-in-law, who knew her so well, had no inkling of the fact. At least Hugo had stated his intention of joining them at Merivale, where she hoped to renew their budding friendship.

"You cannot know what a joy it is to see you dancing with your brother," Harriet remarked at a ball they were attending one evening. Brew had returned Becca to her side and had gone to procure some refreshment for them both. "I remember the first time he danced with me. He'd kept secret from me the fact that he'd been practising and walked with a stick far longer than was necessary so I shouldn't suspect."

"I think perhaps Brew learned to keep his own counsel over the years for fear of betraying his feelings," Becca replied. "But to give you such a surprise — well, if you ask me, it is typical of him. Nothing would give him greater pleasure than to give you pleasure in turn, Harry."

"Then I must tell you he looked more mischievous than anything else, but I do believe he was nervous. In fact, I know he was, for he later told me it was far more daunting than leading his men into battle."

"He's certainly a born campaigner. It is to be hoped that you can exercise some control over him when the baby arrives, for nothing is more certain than that he will immediately be wound around one tiny finger."

Becca's hand was claimed once more and Louisa, who had been engaged with friends, came to sit beside her daughter.

"Are you comfortable, dearest? These chairs are very dainty, but for a woman in your condition they are not the best, I imagine."

Harriet laughed. "I don't know about me, Mama, but your grandchild is wriggling around in protest."

"Would you like me to ask Brew to take you home?" Louisa asked, more concerned than she liked to admit.

"Not at all. What a poor creature you must think me. Perhaps, though, you would walk about the room with me for a few moments to give this child an opportunity to settle down."

"She's doing well, isn't she?" observed Louisa as they passed Becca, who was talking animatedly to her partner on the dancefloor.

"I wish only that she could meet a man to make her as happy as her brother makes me," sighed Harriet. "She hardly mentions what happened last year, but instead of it destroying her confidence, I believe it has been the making of her."

"It's my belief that it's why people are so drawn to her. She has none of the shyness of a debutante, and her easy-going manners must please. She seems entirely unaware of her popularity, and that is an attraction in itself. Will she go with us to Merivale, do you think?"

"You are to come then, Mama? I had thought you might prefer to remain in London after such a long absence."

"And miss the birth of my first grandchild! No, if Becca wishes to remain in town, I can safely leave her to the care of your Aunt Matilda."

Harriet didn't know if her sister-in-law would go with them, for nothing had yet been decided. There was no doubt in Rebecca's own mind that the social whirl suited her admirably, perhaps, she thought, because her earlier life had been so sheltered. But she also wanted to return to the place where she had found herself, had realised she was safe, and had known that nothing could ever be quite so bad again. There was also the small matter of the expectation of seeing Hugo. She raised the question with her brother later that evening, when they had returned to Grosvenor Square and Harriet had retired.

"Have you decided yet when you are to travel into Kent, Brew?"

"Had you asked me yesterday I would have said no, but I have today received a letter from Hugo. He tells me he will be returning next Wednesday, for he hopes to be back in time to join us." Rebecca felt a sudden warmth to know the Frenchman would be with them so soon, but her brother was speaking again. "Just as well, for I would not wish to delay much longer and I know Harriet is eager to be settled there in good time. Do you come with us?"

There was no hesitation. "Of course. How can you even ask?"

Whether her reply would have been the same had his friend not been joining them, she chose not to question.

Hugo had been uncharacteristically subdued as the carriage drove him away from London. He was, after all, much in the habit of waving his arms about and indulging in flowery speeches. But something had changed two nights ago, when he had attended a ball in company with his friends.

"Mademoiselle will do me the honour?" he had smiled seductively, inviting Rebecca to dance with him. She'd laughed in response, already accustomed to his sometimes extravagant manner and apparently liking it above the more decorous ways of her own compatriots.

He'd led her to the floor. It had been a waltz and, as he'd gathered her in his arms, he knew life would never be the same again. No shy young girl in her first season, Becca had confidently allowed herself to be swept about the room. Hugo could only marvel at how well they fitted together. This was not the first time he'd performed the moves, but never before had they been so effortless. When he returned her to Harriet's side, he made his excuses as best he could and retired immediately to the card room. "No doubt I shall find Brew there," he said in an attempt to justify his haste.

He had the right of it and joined the game as another rose to leave. However, his mind wasn't on the task at hand, and his friend raised an eyebrow at an uncommon error. Hugo forced himself to concentrate and it was only overnight, after many wakeful hours, that he decided he must remove himself from temptation. He wanted to leave that very day, but such alacrity would surely have occasioned remark. Instead, he bided his time and was grateful that the object of his despair was out walking for part of the morning and engaged elsewhere in the evening. It was enough to bear that he'd had to sit close by Rebecca at the table for dinner before she went out.

"You are strangely quiet, monsieur. Perhaps something is troubling you?" she'd asked, concern writ all over her face.

"*Mais non*, it is only that I must leave London for a while." He'd addressed the remark to all three of his companions and hoped — though he must not hope, for circumstances did not allow — that there had been a glimmer of disappointment in Becca's eyes. He'd used business as an excuse, but the truth was that he'd fallen hopelessly in love. Hugo had refused the offer of Brew's own carriage, choosing to hire one instead. Though he could not state it, his reason was that at the time he did not know if he would be able to return. With the present state of his affairs, he was not in a position to offer marriage, and might never be able to do so. Better to cut the connection now than cause pain, most certainly to himself and perhaps to Rebecca.

It was early evening by the time he arrived at Kebble Manor, and he cursed himself for a fool at not having recollected that he had put off his people when leaving for France a few years ago. Obviously the place was in darkness, and with only Henri at hand, for he had accompanied him in the coach, it was useless to expect to remain there that night.

"*Merde!*"

The valet remained impassive and awaited further instruction.

"*Imbécile!*"

Henri was confident the expletive had not been directed at him. "May I suggest, monsieur, that we repair to an inn and seek a solution in the morning?"

Hugo grinned, for in spite of his heartache he was blessed with a sense of the ridiculous that could perceive humour in the situation. "An excellent idea. And tomorrow I will contact that man I left in charge; I do not for the moment recall his name…"

"A Mr Standish, I believe."

"What would I do without you, Henri? *Oui*, I will contact Mr Standish and have him hire sufficient staff to maintain our comfort for a few days. Now, if you would, ask the driver to locate an inn for us, and as quickly as possible. I'm starving!"

Accommodation having been secured, Hugo made an excellent meal which did much to restore his good humour and allowed him a good night's sleep. A note had been despatched to the steward prior to his retiring, and that worthy arrived before Hugo had even finished his breakfast. The situation was made light of.

"If you could just while away the morning here, sir, and return to the manor by, shall we say, mid-afternoon, I am confident all will be in place for your comfort. You would wish me to engage a cook as well, of course. Permit me to say how happy I am to have you back amongst us. There will be many in the neighbourhood who will remember you and, of course, your dear departed father, Monsieur Berge."

Hugo had not informed anyone of his changed status when he'd left England, and it came almost as a shock to him to hear his uncle referred to as his parent, but of course it had always been so when they had lived there. He allowed it to pass. Nothing could be served, for the time being, in complicating matters. He found himself impatient to return to what had been his home for so many years, but by dint of hiring a hack he succeeded in passing the time rediscovering once-familiar landmarks and enjoying some cold ham and excellent bread at an out-of-the-way place he'd never before visited. Washing down the remains of his meal with a pint of ale, he then rode directly to Kebble Manor, having arranged that Henri would meet him there with his luggage.

"I have laid out a change of raiment for you, monsieur, and had a quiet word with the cook, just to let her know one or two of your favourites, you understand. It astonishes me how much Mr Standish has achieved so quickly. The rooms have been aired, the dust covers removed and your old bedchamber made ready for you."

It was no part of a valet's job to see to these things, of course, but the two had been together for several years, these past few on the Continent having formed something of an unusual relationship between them. Henri knew, perhaps more than anyone, what torments his master had gone through in his attempts to uncover the fate of his parents. Thus far he had been singularly unsuccessful, but the valet knew that he would not rest until the mystery could be resolved.

With little to occupy himself until the next meal, his excuse that he had business to attend to having been just that, Hugo repaired to the room his uncle had set aside as his personal sanctum. It was a place the young Hugo had known not to enter unless invited, and many a time he had waited with a child's impatience for his 'father' to emerge. He had, of course, investigated it before leaving England. Indeed, it had been the result of his searching that had sent him to France.

He looked around the chamber now, feeling his uncle's presence there, feeling in awe still. It wasn't a large room, but the man's personality was stamped upon it. It couldn't be called a library, only one wall being covered with books. In any case, another room in the house had that designation and Hugo had used it as a schoolroom, Monsieur Berge always preferring the smaller, more intimate space. Hugo walked about slowly, touching a table here, a leather-covered volume there. His movements seemed to be aimless, but finally he seated himself in front of the desk where he had discovered so much that had been secret for so many years. Laying his head on his arms, he wept as he had not done since childhood. Angry with himself for what he considered a weakness, he suddenly sat up straight and banged his fist on the corner. He felt something jar against his knee and bent down to find the source. A small drawer had shot out from behind the conventional top one on the right-hand side. He reached in and slid it out. It came away entirely and he placed it on the top of the desk, excitement mounting at this new discovery.

"*Mon Dieu, qu'est que c'est?*"

It wasn't a large compartment. The normal width of the one that had shielded it, it was barely five inches deep, which was why he'd previously had no idea it was there. There was nothing apparently abnormal about its larger brother. It contained but two letters, and Hugo opened the first with trembling fingers. It was written in French in a hand he didn't recognise. A woman's hand.

Mon Cher Pierre

My heart is breaking. I have lost the love of my life and I have lost my son. Will I ever see either of you again? I think not. Jacques speaks constantly of your bravery in smuggling Hugo out of the country. He says his young brother is an adventurer but will take good care of our boy. I thank the Lord he knows not how much of an adventurer you really are. But we could not help it, could we? I did not ask to fall in love with you, nor you with me. You may imagine both my joy and despair when Jacques showed me your letter and I knew you were both safe.

A mist seemed to drop over Hugo's eyes as he realised the implication of what he was reading. Was Pierre his father after all? He read on.

Little Juliette is now six months old, and I know not if she is yours or my husband's. I have recovered from the illness that afflicted me after her birth, but things are so dangerous here and my little girl too young to travel safely should we need to maintain silence to avoid discovery. And so we remain. It is strange, is it not, that you will be the master of your nephew's fate and your brother the master of a child who may not be his. I will try and write again but, as you may imagine, it is difficult for me to send something in secret. If it were not for my maid, you would not be reading this now.

Remember I love you.
In despair
Yours forever
Isabelle

Hugo turned the letter over, but there was nothing on the back. He stood up and paced the floor in his frustration, but at least one question had been resolved. The man who had raised him was indeed his uncle. But there was a sister of whom he had known nothing. As great a shock as any, that. And who had fathered her? And then he remembered there had been another sheet of paper folded behind the first, and he almost turned the chair over as he rushed to retrieve it.

Mon Cher Pierre

It is as bad as we feared. Worse, even. They will come for us soon, we are sure. Our only hope is for Juliette. If she remains with us, she will surely die. Anne-Marie, my maid, is today to take her into the country. She loves the child as her own and will remove with her to her home village of Sully-sur-Loire, some fourteen or fifteen miles from here. There she will be raised not as her noble status dictates but as a peasant. I care not, just as long as she survives.

Without Anne-Marie to carry my letters away, I have no way of contacting you. When she is gone, you will not know if the worst has happened or if it is only that I am unable to get word to you. Be brave, mon cher.

Isabelle

There was no more. Hugo reached into the cavity to see if anything had fallen out, but there was nothing. He was almost as much in the dark as before. Had his mother survived? Had his father? And what of little Juliette? But no. He did have something. Before, in his search, he'd only had the château. Now he had Anne-Marie. Now he had Sully-sur-Loire!

CHAPTER FOUR

With Hugo's imminent arrival, Rebecca allowed herself to admit she had missed him. He was, after all, a charming and gallant companion. She felt safe with him, as she did with her brother, but no, she definitely did not regard him in the light of a brother. Unable to define her feelings, she put the question aside. What did it matter, after all? Not everything in life had to have an explanation. Lady Sawcroft reiterated Louisa's invitation that she might remain with her in London when the party removed to Merivale, but she declined graciously.

"I am to become an aunt for the first time and wish to be with my family. If you do not consider it presumptuous of me, though, I might like to join you after a while, if Harriet and Brew should remain in Kent for several weeks." She did not question her own motives — did not even consciously consider that a certain Frenchman might do the same.

"You are welcome to stay with me at St James's Square any time, my dear," Matilda said, rapping Becca's knuckles gently with her fan in approval. "Do not betray me to that sister-in-law of mine, but I have become used to company since Louisa came to live with me and will miss her lively presence when she is at Merivale."

Becca laughed. "Impossible not to, I think. She is an extraordinarily amiable lady, and I don't believe I've ever heard her say a bad word about anybody."

It was Lady Sawcroft's turn now to laugh, and she did so with gusto. "It is evident you have not been privileged to be party to one of our tête-à-têtes then. Louisa enjoys a gossip as much as the next person, and I include myself in that," she added before Rebecca could comment. Lady Sawcroft had such an engaging personality that she knew she would be happy to stay with her should the need arise, irrespective of the disparity in their ages, and she was truly grateful.

Hugo was to return to London the following day, and the whole party would leave for Kent on the Friday. With only two weeks to Harriet's confinement Brew was concerned that they had cut things rather fine, but his wife only laughed at him and said that she hoped the jolting of the carriage might promote her going into labour.

"If he jolts the carriage, I shall put the driver off immediately! In fact, perhaps it would be better for your comfort if I drive myself."

"No, please don't do that, Brew. It reassures me to see you through the window, riding beside me where the road provides sufficient width for you to do so, although if Hugo is to ride also I doubt there will be much opportunity."

"It shall be as you wish, my darling," he said, embracing her very carefully, which made her laugh and him in turn. "In any case, I believe from something he said in his letter that he will be travelling independently. Until he arrives, I do not even know if he comes with us on the same day."

"Well, we shall know soon enough. Tomorrow is almost upon us, and it is time I got some sleep."

The comte arrived in the middle of the afternoon, and from his demeanour none would have been able to detect that he had experienced so much emotional upheaval while he'd been away. The truth was, he was desperate to set off again for France to explore this new avenue he'd uncovered, and only good manners prevented him from doing so. Yes, he had gone to Hertfordshire in the belief that he might not return, but

Brew was a good friend and had welcomed him into his home without reservation. It would be ungentlemanly not to accept the invitation that had so generously been given. As for Rebecca, though it would be torture to him, he had to conceal his feelings for her. Unless and until he could find a way of revealing his past, he would not in honour attach himself to anyone. And so it was that he swept into the drawing room where the rest were assembled and made them all an extravagant bow.

"My dearest Harriet, you permit? I see I find you in excellent health. You have lost none of your bloom while I've been away."

She could not but smile warmly in response, such was the effect this man had on most people he met.

He turned to Rebecca. "*Chère* Mademoiselle. Enchanting as always." He made the mistake of looking into her eyes and was nearly undone. Only Brew, slapping him on the shoulder and calling him a rogue, saved him from betraying himself.

"But Major Ware, I am French. What would you?" Everyone laughed and the moment passed, though he determined to be more prepared in future to control his emotions. "And we are to go, all of us, to Merivale the day after tomorrow?"

"Indeed, sir. We will leave early on Friday and collect Mama from St James's Square on the way. The plan is that she, Rebecca and I will travel by coach with Brew riding as an escort beside us. Do you join us in the carriage, or will your bear my husband company?"

"It would give me the greatest pleasure to accompany you ladies, but in truth I must journey in my own conveyance, for I think before too long I must return to France. It makes more sense to head for Dover from Kent than to return to London first."

Rebecca's heart dropped like a stone, for this news was unexpected indeed and somehow she'd felt Hugo would remain amongst them for some time to come. "And may we expect your return to these shores any time soon?" she asked in a voice less robust than usual.

Hugo forced himself to be noncommittal, merely saying that there was much to do but that naturally he hoped to join them again in the future. The tea tray was brought in at that moment and broke the mood. By the time it had been dispensed and handed around both Rebecca and Hugo had themselves well in hand, but in their hearts there was sadness.

It wasn't in the nature of either Rebecca or Hugo to dwell on things they could not change, and the whole party left London in high spirits — none more than Harriet, who hadn't seen her former home since before her marriage.

"If you need to halt somewhere overnight you must let me know, my dearest. Don't allow your eagerness to return to Merivale to colour your judgement," Brew said to his wife as they paused to collect Mrs Lambert and load her luggage.

"Don't worry, my boy. If my daughter doesn't show sense, I can assure you I certainly shall," Louisa said before urging him to mount his horse so they could be on their way. "The sooner we leave, the sooner we shall arrive."

As it transpired, the day was entirely uneventful, though tedious. Having discussed the matter previously, it had been decided not to break the journey other than to change horses and the day was much advanced by the time the Wares' carriage swept into the drive, followed closely by Hugo, who had maintained an even distance behind them all the way. As Brew aided his wife and mother-in-law to alight, Hugo gave Rebecca his hand on the other side of the vehicle. Her fingers trembled in his and she stumbled on the steps. He caught her by the elbows and lifted her to the ground.

"You are unwell?" he asked, deeply concerned.

"Not at all," she replied, covering her confusion with an excuse. "After sitting for so many hours in one position, I had not realised that I had cramp. It has passed now. I am grateful to you for saving me, for I would surely otherwise have fallen."

"It is my pleasure to serve you," he said, managing to smile now that he was assured of her safety, though holding her in his arms, albeit fleetingly, had done little for his composure. "Are you ready to join the others?"

"Most certainly, for I wish to reacquaint myself with the house."

"You've been here before?"

"I stayed with Harriet for a short time before her marriage to my brother. It is a delightful place, as I'm sure you will agree."

They turned to face the house. There was no evidence of the previous year's fire and as they mounted the marble steps, they saw only an edifice made of stone that was pleasing to the eye. In the large entrance hall they found, in addition to the travellers, Mrs Sweet, the housekeeper, who assured them that all had been made ready, and Pru, Brew's own childhood nurse who, having waited impatiently for six days following her arrival from Lincolnshire, had come to claim her charge and bear her off to her bedchamber to rest. In the time it took for the others to be escorted to their allocated rooms and reassemble again in the drawing room, Rebecca and Hugo had both recovered their fortitude and were able to behave in their usual manner. Only Harriet was missing.

"I hope my sister-in-law is well, Brew. It seemed to me that she was displaying signs of fatigue for the last few miles, for she was unusually quiet and some of her enthusiasm seemed to have waned."

"Merely tired and ready to obey Nurse's command that she lie on her bed for an hour or two. She'd expressed a wish to see the results of the reparations but in a half-hearted sort of way, and when Pru insisted she wait until later there was no argument."

"Reparations?" Hugo enquired.

"Yes, there was a fire last year and one wing of the house had to be restored entirely. I wouldn't mind a look myself. Would you care to join me?"

The two men left the room and Louisa addressed Rebecca with some concern. "You are not distressed, my dear?"

Rebecca turned a warm smile upon her, knowing she was referring to her previous misfortunes. "Not at all. Though I was frightened when I first arrived, it seems so long ago now and my memories of this place are all good ones. It was here that I recovered my strength and, to some extent, my self-respect."

"You had gone through a terrible ordeal."

"And had it not been for Harriet and Gil, my story might have had quite another ending."

"Yes, Gil is an admirable young man," Louisa said fondly.

"I keep forgetting he too is your son-in-law. Naturally I see much of him and Amabel when at home, as they live so close to Austerly."

"Yes, my one regret is that my own home is so far away and that I see so little of both my daughters. Not that I repine, for I am truly happy living with Lady Sawcroft and it suits me far more than Merivale ever did. What my husband and Harriet always saw in the place I shall never know."

"But it is a charming house."

"It was never the house but rather the location. Not that Percival ever knew, nor the girls, I think, until sometime after his death. Anyway," she said, giving herself a little shake as the memory of her late husband threatened to overcome her, "my understanding is that Amabel and Gil are so content that they may forego a trip to London this season. It is as yet undecided."

"They said nothing to me before I left home. I wouldn't despair of seeing them, though. Both are, I believe, of an impulsive nature."

"That much is certain."

Hugo and Brew returned a few moments later and conversation turned to the building works, which had very much impressed the major.

The next morning Harriet admitted to still feeling fatigued so Brew, Rebecca and Hugo cast aside their guilt and went riding. A number of horses had been sent down from Lincolnshire, Brew having previously anticipated that they might spend several weeks in Kent and wanting to have his own cattle there. Thus was his sister privileged to ride Brandy, one of his wife's favourites, while he and Hugo too were suitably mounted. With the advance of spring there was a slight softening to the bleak landscape that lay behind the estate. Brew had covered the area to a degree the previous year, and though he was not entirely familiar with it he was able to demonstrate to his companions how different it was to anything they'd seen before. A good gallop was found to be a tonic to them all.

"I feel I have shaken off my fidgets from sitting so long in a carriage yesterday," Becca remarked as they walked from the stables back to the house they had left three hours earlier. It had had a beneficial effect on Hugo also, although he was finding it increasingly difficult not to hasten to France to continue his investigations. Leaving Rebecca behind would be hard. Remaining in her company was also hard. In any case, sheer good manners dictated he stay a few days longer.

Entering the house through the back, they repaired to the drawing room to announce their return, only to find Louisa sitting alone and leafing through some fashion plates she had brought with her from London. She looked up as they came in.

"It would seem that like its mother, your child is in a hurry, Brew. In your absence Harriet's labour has begun."

He paled and gripped the back of a chair. "But it is too soon! The baby is not due for another two weeks."

Louisa laughed. "It is fortunate these things are left in the hands of women. I should not have guessed it of you, my boy. You are normally so calm and in control. A few days either way will make little difference, and it could be many hours yet. Possibly not even until tomorrow. No, don't go rushing off," she added as he started for the door. "Nurse will not allow you anywhere near. I myself have been banished, as you can see."

Brew began to pace and Louisa turned to Hugo, who had moved with Rebecca to stand by the window. "For goodness' sake, take him off somewhere. Go and change your clothes and have something to eat, and maybe you could go out later and try for some rabbits."

"I couldn't eat a mouthful," replied her agitated son-in-law.

Louisa merely raised an eyebrow and Hugo bore his friend off, leaving Becca to ask anxiously, "Is it true that these two weeks are not significant?"

"I should have preferred her to go full term, of course, but I daresay yesterday's journey might have something to do with this early onset. Perhaps we should have come sooner and broken the journey overnight. And don't you go repeating that to your brother, for it might have made no difference at all and we can see he isn't going to be handling this well."

Rebecca was reassured, but in truth Louisa was more concerned than she was admitting. She'd acquiesced to Nurse's request that she remove herself, acknowledging that to be having the fidgets would do her daughter no good and that holding her hand would serve little purpose.

Brew and Louisa had both knocked on the door at different times during the course of the afternoon and Nurse, the ruler of her domain, had allowed them entry, raising a finger to her lips on both occasions. "She is sleeping for the moment and needs all her strength, so don't you go waking her."

Louisa had assured her she wouldn't dream of doing so. Brew, who had managed to cajole Nurse since a child, did not meet with his usual success. He was told in no uncertain terms that he should have her to answer to if he upset her charge. Unfortunately for him, Harriet came awake suddenly as a sharp pain caused her to cry out.

"Now, don't you fret, Master Brew. Just hold her hand for a while until the pain subsides. It's perfectly normal."

It seemed that his voice soothed his wife, for she settled fairly soon. He'd been shocked to see her in so much discomfort, and Nurse ushered him out of the room before another episode should occur. In these circumstances, he was most certainly not an asset.

Dinner that evening was a strange affair, and it was Hugo who held everything together.

"Are we taking bets, *mon ami*? A girl or a boy?"

Brew wasn't proof against the charming smile that told him his friend was joking, though he said seriously, "I just pray for a safe delivery."

"You have discussed names, no?"

In fact they hadn't, and Hugo came up with some outrageous suggestions that brought some amusement to the rest.

"How about Balthasar? Or Ebenezer? Hezekiah, perhaps? Or maybe Zedekiah? Now, there are some good biblical names."

"Which you know how?" Brew asked with a faint smile.

"You forget, I was brought up in this country. My uncle made sure I followed the Scriptures."

"And what if it's a girl?" asked Rebecca.

"Well, yours is a beautiful biblical name," he replied, caught off guard for a moment. He recovered well. "What do you think of Hepzibah? Vashti? Zipporah? Now, there's a lovely name. It means bird."

Brew said he was astonished at Hugo's knowledge, to which he replied, "There is much about me you don't know. Of course, there is also much about myself I do not know."

This latter remark covered a truth but in the context it served to amuse the others, and so the evening passed with Brew managing at least to give the appearance of calm. But as they all retired for the night, there was as yet no news from upstairs.

CHAPTER FIVE

The next morning brought no change. Leaving Harriet's room, where she had slept on a truckle bed, Nurse went to refresh herself and stretch her aching limbs. "I am not as young as I used to be, Mrs Sweet," she confided to the housekeeper, "and my bones are telling me so. Not that I would dream of telling the mistress, and nor must you. A little walk will soon put me to rights again."

"How is the poor dear doing? Would you like me to go and sit with her? I used to be able to comfort her when she was a child, if she fell off her pony or some such thing."

"No, for her mama is with her and thankfully she is sleeping. I hope she gets some respite, for she has had a difficult night. I'll go and find the rest of the family now," she added and went to the drawing room. Brew jumped up but wasn't surprised to learn that there was no news. He had visited his wife's room a while ago, before being bustled away by Nurse with the comment, "You always were a restive lad, Master Brew. Off you go now. This is no place for a man." He was no match for Pru, particularly when she invoked memories of his childhood. "Master Hugo, do take this jumble of nerves for a ride or perhaps to fish in the stream, from where he can be fetched if needs be. And you, Miss Rebecca, will do me the favour of walking with me in the garden before I go back upstairs."

Satisfied that she had organised her troops, Pru's plans proceeded as she had appointed and the two men went off to find some fishing tackle.

The calmness of the river worked its magic and somehow Brew controlled his restlessness, remarking to his friend, "We have had little opportunity to talk since you returned from Hertfordshire, Hugo. What found you there?"

The Frenchman was a little surprised at such acuity. "What makes you think I found anything?"

"I know you well, and though I have been tied up in my own affairs I could not help but notice a change in you. An unease that was not there before you went. Was there indeed something?" Brew was familiar with the details of Hugo's past, insofar at least as he was aware of them himself.

"I discovered a hidden drawer in my uncle's desk. It contained two letters." He paused and drew in a deep breath. "From my mother."

"Good heavens, man, some more information? Something you can go on?"

"Not as much as I would have wished, *mais oui*, there was sufficient for me to investigate where I have not before. I will show you the letters if you wish, when we get back to the house. I have no secrets from you." *None, except that I'm in love with your sister*, he thought.

"You are anxious to leave, I can tell."

"I am, but I would not go at such a time. After all, I am eager to know which of the biblical names I suggested you will choose for your child," he said, laughing and jerking his rod, thus definitely disturbing any fish that might have been in the vicinity. Brew jumped up once more and declared he could sit still no longer. "It would have been better if we'd gone shooting, for this inactivity suits me not at all. I fear I must drag you back, Hugo. Forgive me."

But Hugo too was fidgety and had no objection to being on the move. They were shocked at what they found. Nurse was standing in the hall with Mrs Sweet looking grave, and they heard her ask for Brew to be fetched. He startled her, coming in suddenly, and demanded to know what was amiss.

"Ah, good, you are here. Things are not progressing as well as I would have wished. I think perhaps it is time we sent for the doctor."

"Just give me his direction and I will go for him myself," Brew said at once.

"It would perhaps be preferable that I go, and you may give comfort to Harriet if you are able," offered Hugo.

This time Nurse did not protest. She bore Brew upstairs as Hugo asked the footman to send for the carriage and Mrs Sweet explained to him where he might find the doctor. Fortunately Dr Allen was found at home and that worthy, at first suspicious of a 'foreigner', made haste to fetch his bag when he heard Mrs Ware was to be his patient. As a child he'd admired Harriet's intrepidity, and had set a broken bone and tended her other ailments. He leapt into the carriage with more agility than one might expect from a man of his age, and they were back at Merivale only an hour after Hugo had left.

Dr Allen was shown upstairs, and paused outside Harriet's door before knocking gently. Nurse slipped out into the corridor to tell him of the progress, or lack thereof, that was being made and that her patient was by now exhausted and very weak. He frowned and followed her back inside, addressing Brew as he came to greet him.

"You are the father?"

"Yes, sir."

"Well, there's no call for you to look so down in the mouth. We'll have you celebrating soon enough. Off you go now, and leave this to me and the nurse here."

His cheery tone did much to raise Brew's spirits, but in fact the doctor was concerned about the length of the confinement, though he pasted a smile upon his face as he moved towards the bed.

"Just like you to be creating a fuss, is it not, Harriet? Let's see what's to do here, so that you may be comfortable again."

He was rewarded with a wan smile. "It's hurts so, Dr Allen."

"It's not surprising that any child of yours would be wanting to make a grand entrance, now, is it?"

Harriet smiled again, but it was a poor effort. Upon examination, he confirmed immediately what Nurse had suspected was the problem. The babe was not presenting in the normal way, and its mother had been exerting herself without possibility of a happy outcome.

"Now, don't you worry yourself any, but I'm going to have to give you some help here. I'll just get some implements from my bag and I'm sure we'll be done in no time."

He'd always been able to reassure her, and his tone now sounded full of a confidence he didn't entirely feel. However, experience was on his side and with some manipulation and a final supreme effort by Harriet, she was in a short while safely delivered of her child. Nurse bustled about, assisting. As a result of the infant's cries, the door was flung open and its father burst into the room. Pru, who was about to lay the baby on its mother's breast, instead handed it to a somewhat nervous Brew.

"It's a girl," she said. "You have a daughter."

Brew looked down upon the child with awe, and tears ran from his eyes. He moved towards the bed where his wife was smiling, and he sat beside her and laid the baby down.

"Nancy," she said.

"Yes, Nancy." And though they had never discussed names, he knew that his long-gone sister would be remembered in this child.

Celebrations were short-lived when it became obvious that Harriet's life was in danger. She'd lost a huge amount of blood, and Dr Allen was of the opinion that it would take an effort on the part of all those caring for her to pull her through. He gave strict instructions that Nurse Pru, Rebecca and especially Louisa should spend only limited time with her, taking turns so they might rest in between. He wanted to make sure they were all alert enough not to miss any changes and strong enough to do what was necessary. "You will be of little use to her if you are yourselves exhausted." He prescribed various remedies and needed to be certain they would be administered. Of Nurse he had no doubt, but Mrs Lambert, whom he had known for many years, had crumbled before them all. He had little knowledge of Rebecca, though she seemed capable enough.

"Major Ware, I would be less than honest if I didn't advise you that in my opinion, things are grave. Grave indeed. Your infant is thriving and I see no reason why she should not continue to do so, but I am more concerned for your wife than I care to say. However, I know her for a fighter. If anyone can make it through this, it is Harriet."

"Just tell me what to do, Doctor," Brew answered quietly but firmly.

"Well, that's just it, Major. I am of the opinion that the best thing is for you to do nothing. I make no doubt that as a leader of men, you were most capable in your job. In the sick room you are not, and the more time you spend there the more distressed your wife will be."

Brew was shocked, but when he thought about it he believed he understood. "You think Harriet will be adversely affected? That I will have a detrimental effect upon her recovery?"

"You put it harshly, but yes; it is my belief that she will put strength she does not have to spare into reassuring you. It is of paramount importance that every ounce of energy she has is concentrated upon herself. My suggestion is that you visit her each morning and evening, for perhaps five minutes, for she would think it strange if you did not come to her at all, and that would only cause her to fret."

"Yes, I see."

"Occupy yourself as best you can in between times. That will help you and in turn aid your wife. I will come each day to visit, so you may save any questions for then, rather than send for me in a panic. On the other hand, don't hesitate to call for me if you feel the need. I'll bid you good day now, Major."

Dr Allen left, and Brew was left wondering how he was to know what constituted a need. Nurse would tell him, he was sure. She was at present sitting with Harriet and would have received instructions directly from the doctor, so he went to report to the others who were, he knew, waiting anxiously in the drawing room for news.

"It is time for a gallop across this strange landscape you have brought me to," Hugo said immediately after his friend had imparted the new information. "It is what is called for to divert you."

Brew, his sensitivities close to the surface, said somewhat coldly that he neither required nor wanted to have his thoughts diverted away from his wife. It was Rebecca who said, "I'm sure that's not what Hugo meant. Pru will soon require some respite, and I will go and sit with my sister-in-law. Louisa will in turn follow me, will you not?" she said, looking at her enquiringly. Poor Mrs Lambert seemed desolate, but everyone knew that she would hide these feelings when time came for her to be with her daughter. "There is nothing you can do for the next few hours, so do as has been suggested, Brew. It may be that you can persuade Harriet to take some gruel, or whatever it is the doctor has prescribed. She will make the effort for you, I am certain, where she may not for the rest of us."

This was an inspired suggestion, for it made him feel he might be useful. No lighter of heart but with at least the hope of being of some help, Brew allowed Hugo to lead him away.

"He is handsome, is he not?" Louisa asked, summoning a smile as she watched Rebecca's gaze follow the men from the room. "Be careful, dearest. I should not want to see you hurt again."

Rebecca tore her gaze from the door. "No, you mistake. Well, not about his being handsome, I mean, but my affections are not engaged."

"He is restless, that one. Something troubles him, and I do not think he will remain with us long."

Becca had felt it too. She had tried so hard to be on her guard, but he had crept in beneath her defences. No matter. Time had taught her to be strong. Soon she would return to London and continue the social whirl she enjoyed so much. She couldn't understand why the idea seemed not to appeal to her. She set aside thoughts of herself and said she must go to Harriet.

"I will come with you and sit a while with Nancy in the dressing room. There can be no objection, surely, and I will be on hand should you need me."

"Ought you not to be resting yourself? For later, you understand, when it is your turn."

"I cannot. You will understand when you have children of your own."

Rebecca gave up the argument and they went together up the stairs. The doctor had earlier despatched a wet nurse from the village to Merivale, who had fortunately gained the approval of Pru. She was happy to hand the infant to her grandmamma, and Louisa sat contentedly cradling Nancy in her arms while in the room next door Becca fought hard to control her emotions at the sight of Harriet. Her usual cream complexion seemed parched and her sister-in-law suppressed the urge to call for Nurse, knowing she would not have left her charge in the first place if there had been cause for greater anxiety. She sat by the bed and took Harriet's hand in her own. It felt dry. Her eyes flickered open and there was a slight pressure in return.

"Rebecca. Dearest sister. I fear I have made a mull of things, have I not?"

"You have had a difficult time, for sure, but your baby is thriving. It only remains for you to put all your strength into getting well again."

"She is beautiful, is she not?" At last a smile.

"Indeed she is. But I have been told you are not to tax yourself with trying to talk. Be assured that I shall sit with you until your mother comes to take my place. You have only to move your hand to call for my attention. The best thing for you now is to sleep."

She rather suspected that Harriet had already fallen into slumber before she'd finished speaking. Becca was left alone with her thoughts. They were mixed. She remembered the first time she'd danced with Hugo. It was something she thought about often, for she had begun to realise even then that her heart was lost to him. When he had gone away to Hertfordshire, a piece of her had been missing until his return.

These feelings were not to be compared with what she had experienced all those months ago at the hands of her would-be abductor. Then she had thought herself in love. Now she realised what a difference there was between that emotion and infatuation. The latter could be recovered from. But this?

Hugo was in a state of anxiety on many levels. As he and Brew cantered together, he had little appreciation for the landscape, as his thoughts were turned inwards. His mount was content to run shoulder to shoulder with his companion, so a light hand on the rein was all he required. One brief glance sideways was sufficient for him to be satisfied his friend's mind was also not occupied by Nature's beauty. The frown was visible even at this angle and distance.

The comte turned his mind to his own problems. The need to take off for France increased in urgency as each day passed. What of his sister? Was she aware she had a brother? Did she know of her antecedents, or did she believe herself to be born to a different class entirely? Were their mother and father alive still? He could hope, but he could not believe. Had his uncle not designated him Comte du Berge? Would he not have been Vicomte, had Pierre truly believed in the survival of his own brother? It had been years since he'd had any new evidence, but now…? Armed with the information contained in the two letters from his mother to his uncle, Hugo could hardly wait to go.

When he and Brew had met in France some four or so years ago, both had been at a low ebb. Chance had led them to the same card table and when the evening was over they'd continued together, a bottle of wine for company, and then another. Each had had problems of a family nature, and it wasn't long before they'd begun to exchange confidences. The major had been supportive, and Hugo would not leave him now when such loyalty was required in return.

His horse leapt forward apace as the rider's legs inadvertently pressed against its flanks. Cursing himself, Hugo brought him back and would have fallen again into reflection but that Brew turned to him and smiled. It transformed him. "Apollo is eager, I see. What say you we give them a gallop?"

"*D'accord*. A race, perhaps?"

Brew laughed. It was good to hear, and Hugo's own mood lifted. They set off somewhat recklessly, neither familiar with the terrain, but the possibility of hidden ditches or other hazards only added to the enjoyment of the chase. There being no ultimate goal, neither was declared the winner, but both felt better for the challenge. As they walked back towards Merivale, their horses now on a loose rein, Brew voiced his anxiety.

"I was never so fearful on the battlefield. Harriet is so pale. So quiet. And she lost so much blood. I don't know what I would do without her!"

"You despair too quickly, *mon ami*. You have many times witnessed the strength of the human spirit and your wife, she has so much to live for. You must not let her see you with such a grave face."

"No, of course not, but I've never felt so helpless. What can I do?"

"You are a leader of men, Brew. When you are with her, your authority will assert itself. And your determination will transmit itself and make Harriet all the more resolved to get better. And she has a child to think of, too. It will add to her firmness of purpose." He could see that speaking of the infant was having a beneficial effect and continued. "It was *très amusant* playing with names the other day, but you have chosen well. Nancy is much more agreeable than any of my suggestions. And your parents? Will they not be pleased with your choice?"

By gentle cajoling and a little bullying, Hugo succeeded in raising his friend's spirits so that by the time they reached the house, he was able to visit his wife in a far more positive frame of mind. Hugo, retiring to his own room for a while, dismissed his valet and revisited his own problems. Of the happenings in Sully-sur-Loire, he could only speculate. Anxious as he was, there was no way he would leave his friend at this time. By all accounts, the situation in France was stable for the time being and he had to place his dependence upon that not changing until he could go back.

He returned to contemplation of Rebecca and smiled involuntarily. She was never far from his thoughts, but his smile was chased away by a frown at this helplessness. Every muscle, every sinew longed to take her in his arms, to declare his undying love for her. But Hugo had been born and raised a gentleman. Until his family problems were resolved, he knew not what he could offer her. He had funds enough, for sure, but money was not everything in this world. More important to him was position, and until he knew what that was he could say nothing. There were so many secrets in his past. When he left, as he assuredly must before too long, he would go without any claim upon her. He knew of her plan to return to London. Such a beautiful woman must surely be much courted, and perhaps won. Would she be free when he returned? He groaned, went down to the drawing room and fixed a smile upon his face before entering.

He found Rebecca alone in the room. He was surprised and it took him a moment to recover. Then he recalled that Louisa was probably still sitting with her daughter, or taking some time to rest if Brew or Nurse were in attendance. Becca was standing by the window, a simple muslin gown serving to highlight the contours of her fine figure. She was gazing out at something in the distance, or perhaps at nothing at all. He could not know. He didn't want to alarm her, so he took a step back and rapped gently to announce his presence. She broke her gaze and turned her head towards him, and a smile of pure sweetness suffused her features.

"You startled me," she said. "I was daydreaming. Forgive me."

"*Chère Mademoiselle, je suis dèsolé, je te prie de me pardoner.*" Hugo stopped, realising he had lapsed into his native tongue. "I am sorry. I had no thought of confounding you. Would you wish me to withdraw?"

"Of course not. Tell me, how was your ride? Were you able to set my brother's mind at rest?" She moved to sit on a settee with a high back covered in a pale gold fabric and he was distracted for a moment, thinking only of how well it matched the colour of her hair. "Will you not be seated, sir?"

Hugo chose a chair a little apart from where she was seated, unable to trust himself if he came too near, but his voice was steady enough as he replied, "As to that, I think his mind will only be at ease when there is an improvement in Harriet's condition. My understanding is that she is gravely ill."

"I'm afraid that is the case, but the doctor seemed confident that with the right care, she would recover."

"Then we must pray for her. As for Brew, at least he was able to rid himself of an excess of energy — and he was, I think, calmer when we parted. His intention was to change his clothes and go straight to her room. And if he is a little less anxious, then so too will she be, *n'est ce pas*? And here he is," Hugo added, turning to look over his shoulder as Brew appeared at the door.

With a softness of expression that Hugo had never seen in him before, Brew said, "I should like to introduce you to my daughter. Nancy, may I present to you Hugo, Comte du Berge." Rebecca had of course already seen the baby when attending to Harriet. She looked on fondly and then with great gladness as her brother said, "Monsieur le Comte, my wife and I beg you will do us the honour of becoming our daughter's godfather."

Hugo was both surprised and delighted. "Mine is the honour, my friend, and I should of course be more than happy to do so. You are aware, though, that I must soon return to France."

"Of course, but not permanently, I hope."

Hugo shrugged. "I know not. Until I see how things stand, I am unable to make any future commitment." He was in truth imparting a message to Rebecca also, hoping she understood, not knowing if she returned his feelings. He tried to tell himself that it didn't signify, and that it would be better if she hadn't developed a tendre. It would be kinder to her. But he was only fooling himself. The truth was that he would leave happier if he knew she cared for him. He took the risk of looking in her direction, but her eyes were upon Nancy and he couldn't see them to read their expression. He squared his shoulders. "But if I am to be this child's godfather, I beg to make the most of my time with her. You permit?" he asked, holding out his arms to take her from her father. Cradling her, he gently moved the covering away from her face to reveal little tufts of soft hair, the same shade as Brew and Rebecca's. Something tore at his insides as a tiny fist curled itself around his little finger.

Two days later, Dr Allen declared Harriet to be out of danger. "But she has a long way to go, Major Ware, and I suggest you adhere strictly to the regime I have prescribed."

Brew promised to do whatever it might take to hasten his wife's recovery, only to be told, "Hasten is an inappropriate word under the circumstances. However, spring is advancing nicely now, and if the days are sufficiently warm it will do her no harm to recline out of doors in the sunshine for half an hour or so."

"Would today be suitable, do you think? She is talking of her desire to be up and about again."

"It's typical of Harriet that she is starting to feel impatient. She was ever thus, even as a child. However, it is a sign that things are improving. Yes, by all means bring her downstairs. On no account, though, must you permit her enthusiasm or yours to allow her to do too much. Half an hour. No more."

Everything changed from that moment. Harriet, determined to get better, was a surprisingly good patient. When she wasn't on the terrace, she had moved to a day bed in her dressing room, where all but Hugo vied for the privilege of reading to her. He was, however, permitted to visit, and he thanked her for the honour she and her husband had bestowed upon him. For the time that he was allowed to remain, he entertained her by paying her outrageous compliments and behaving in an altogether Gallic manner which delighted her hugely and, more to the point, did her a world of good. At the end of the week, he took his leave of them.

Hugo had found no opportunity to contrive to be alone with Rebecca and, even had he been able to do so, he would not have spoken of his feelings. He could offer her nothing, after all. The hand that trembled in his as he kissed her fingertips gave him hope, and that was all he had to carry with him.

CHAPTER SIX

Rebecca was inconsolable after Hugo left, though none of her companions would have suspected it and no-one enquired too deeply. The happenings of the previous year had taught her to conceal her deepest emotions, but alone in her room she allowed the tears to fall. Had she imagined the connection between them? She thought about the occasional glance, the increased pressure on her hand, the care with which he'd placed a shawl about her shoulders — so many little things that had convinced her he had returned her affections. But he'd said nothing, his parting words to her holding no greater significance than those to the rest. *I made too much of it*, she berated herself, pacing to and fro in her agitation. *Did he not flagrantly flirt with Harriet to lift her spirits? And who is to say he will return? He made no such promise. I must, I will forget him.* At which her tears began to fall once more. Her redemption began the next day, when she received a letter from her mother.

My Darling Rebecca

I can wait no longer to see my granddaughter. Your brother tells me she has the look of a Ware, but I must come and see for myself. Papa, though he would like to join me, is not fit to make the journey, especially as it is my intention to go with you to London from Merivale when my visit there is at an end. Never tell him I told you, but Papa wept when he learned that the child was to be called Nancy. How is the dashing Frenchman? I cannot wait to meet him.

Becca was shaken for a moment. It would seem she had mentioned Hugo too often in her own communications home.

My luggage is already packed and I have written also to Brew, advising him to expect me. By the time you receive this, I shan't be many hours away. You cannot know how excited I am. How much we have to talk about!

Mama

Elizabeth Ware was enchanted by Nancy, and for the first two days she could hardly speak of anything else. The rest of the party indulged her, encouraged her, and even added their own words of adoration. She had been shocked to see how weak her daughter-in-law had become.

"You left me in rude health and high spirits only a few weeks ago. How is it that you've become so frail?" Elizabeth asked, unable to refrain from expressing her concern.

Harriet laughed. Not wishing to alarm his mother, Brew's letters had said little of his wife's confinement or the danger she had been in. "You make me sound like an old lady. I can assure you I am truly on the mend. You have only to ask Nurse. You know her well enough to be sure she would wrap me in wool and shield me from every puff of wind. Now, tell me what you think of your granddaughter."

It needed no more and Elizabeth was diverted, but she later recalled her concern when speaking to Rebecca.

"I was greatly dismayed, I can tell you. Why did no-one warn me? I was foolish enough to draw attention to her appearance, which I'm sure did her no good at all. I just blurted it out. No young lady likes to be told she's looking peaky."

Becca laughed. "Don't fret, Mama. Harriet knows you well enough and, in any case, she is so much improved that I think your words could not have a detrimental effect."

"It's to be hoped so. Now, what of you, my darling? We've had hardly a moment alone since I arrived, and I don't hesitate to tell you that I find you too are not in your best looks. Now, would you listen to me — am I not doing to you the very thing I did to Harriet?"

"Well, if I do appear pinched, you may put it down to worrying about my sister-in-law and keeping strange hours as we took turns to sit with her."

Elizabeth looked directly at her daughter, and Becca knew better than to turn away. She held her mother's gaze as steadily as she was able but, unseen, she was biting the inside of her lip. Not deceived for a moment, Elizabeth made no further enquiries. No-one could ever have accused Mrs Ware of being a fool. Inwardly she wept for her daughter, but when she spoke it was to ask how long she planned to remain at Merivale. "I know from your letters before you came that you were having a fine time in London, and I must say I long to go there myself."

"Now that Harriet is on the mend, I shall feel quite easy about leaving. In fact, the house has been so overrun with people that I suspect our hosts would welcome some time to themselves, not that my brother would ever say so."

"Will Louisa come to town also, do you think?"

"No, it is my belief she will want to remain with her daughter a while longer, until she is well and truly on her feet. We must remember too that Merivale was her home until recently, and she must be comfortable here."

And so it was that the two of them went to London, and for Rebecca it seemed that Hugo was further away than ever.

When Rebecca had returned to town from Merivale a year ago, she'd barely begun the process of recovery from her recent betrayal. As the coach approached the city, she found herself feeling just as wretched, though there was no question of betrayal on this occasion. Perhaps she had misinterpreted a look or a gesture. Nothing had been said, and no promises had been made. Therefore, nothing had been taken from her, and yet she had never felt a loss so deeply. Even when her sister had perished all those years ago, she had been too emotionally immature to understand. And now she had to pretend all was well, and that she was excited to once more enter society with all the delights it had to offer. That her mother hadn't mentioned Hugo told its own story. Least said, soonest mended would be Elizabeth's maxim.

They arrived in Grosvenor Square just as dusk was settling, and it was agreed that they would each retire to their rooms and meet again at supper time. While Becca was left alone with her thoughts, her mother wasted no time in penning a note to Matilda, whom she knew had a fondness for her daughter.

My dear Lady Sawcroft

I hope you do not mind me writing to you to let you know that I am come to town with my daughter, having left Louisa to remain for a while in Kent. Rebecca has told me of your kind offer to house her should your sister-in-law not return. At the time there was no certainty that I would be able to come to London, but I'm happy to say that we are, the two of us, residing for the time being in my son's house in Grosvenor Square. I should like to thank you for your graciousness towards Rebecca and will visit you tomorrow so I may do so in person, as I know she will want to do herself.

Yours,

Elizabeth Ware

There, Elizabeth thought, *that should set the ball rolling.* She had rarely visited London herself and her hope was that Lady Sawcroft, a well-known figure in society, would oil the wheels for them. She was not to be disappointed. The next day, they were sitting in Lady Sawcroft's parlour.

"How delightful to see you again, Mrs Ware. Such a difficult time poor Harriet has had… You must understand that Louisa wrote to tell me all about it. I am happy to learn that things have improved and she is recovering well. Now, young lady," she continued, turning to Rebecca, "I have become a little lazy of late, and you are just what I need to stir me out of my indolence. I shall hold a soirée to which you must both come, and perhaps a visit to the theatre. I keep my own box there, you know. It will not be long before you receive more invitations than there will be sufficient time to fulfil, I am sure."

Elizabeth expressed her gratitude, but their hostess said frankly, "I am aware that you have little acquaintance in London, and it would be a crime indeed if we didn't give your daughter every chance to establish herself. She is a beautiful young lady and will take well, I know. I was surprised you didn't manage to turn her off last season, but we must not despair. There will be opportunities aplenty, and I suggest we begin — while I am making arrangements for the soirée, you understand — by going to the park tomorrow. It is an activity I enjoy and one of *the* places to be seen. I shall send my carriage to collect you."

Rebecca was acutely uncomfortable at being spoken about in this way, but she appreciated what Lady Sawcroft was trying to do for her. Matilda may have had a waspish tongue, but she had a heart of gold. And now it seemed that she must put all thoughts of Hugo aside and enter the fray.

Lady Sawcroft was not one to allow the grass to grow beneath her feet, and in no time it seemed Rebecca had barely a moment to herself, her thoughts of Hugo confined to those few moments of reflection allowed her when she was alone. But Miss Ware had a zest for life that would not long be subdued. In addition, her mood was lifted by the arrival in town of Mr and Mrs Carstairs. They were her neighbours in Lincolnshire; Gil was her lifelong friend and Amabel was Harriet's sister. Unaware of their proposed visit, for they had made a last-minute decision to journey south and had informed no-one, Rebecca was overjoyed when they called upon her and Elizabeth on the day following their arrival.

"Amabel! I had no notion you were coming to town. What a lovely surprise. Unless … there is nothing wrong, I trust?"

"Nothing at all, Becca. With you, Harriet and Brew gone from home, we found we were missing the company of all of you. Gil, finding me a trifle dejected, insisted on bringing me to join you." She turned to Elizabeth while at the same time searching in her reticule. "Cornelius charged me with delivering this letter to you with the instruction to tell you that he is missing his wife, which I considered to be very sweet, but that you should not indulge in a moment's anxiety and only give yourself over to your enjoyment."

They all laughed and Elizabeth, laying the letter on a small table at her side to be read later, said, "What a fraud he is, to be sure, when we all know he will be going about the estate and engaging with our tenants and will barely give me a second thought. He is so much more content since Brew returned and started putting all to rights. My husband is never happier than when finding some previously unseen innovation and has such a pride in Austerly that was lacking before."

"And doubtless you have come to visit your tailor, Gil," Becca added, unable to keep the grin from her face, for clothes were his weakness, not that he would regard it as such. While her brother and Hugo (she was as yet unable to banish him from her thoughts) both dressed in an elegant but understated manner, Gil liked nothing more than to indulge his sartorial taste for bright colours and flamboyant accessories. Today he was wearing yellow pantaloons and a waistcoat of the same colour, decorated with a dark green thread that exactly matched his coat.

"How well you understand me, Becca," he said, giving her an exaggerated bow. "But it is not only me. My wife also wishes to replenish her wardrobe. And I believe we shall take some time to travel into Kent to meet our niece."

Amabel frowned fleetingly. "How is my sister, Becca? Tell me truly."

"You may be assured she is recovering her health now and is making great progress — is that not so, Mama?"

"Indeed, else we should not have left her. As you are aware, she is in the care of your mother and Nurse Pru. I defy anyone not to get better in their hands."

"And your son, Elizabeth?"

"Never before was there a child like this one. Poor man, he is besotted."

Amabel was reassured, and of course Rebecca and her mother would not be in such high spirits if there was anything amiss. The women arranged a time to go shopping the very next day but in fact met again that evening, Lady Sawcroft having invited them to join her theatre party when she'd been informed of their arrival. Elizabeth, observing her daughter and Amabel with their heads together and chatting amiably, could only hope that the presence of their friends would be another distraction. Too often did she see such a bleak look in Becca's eyes as to break her heart.

It wasn't in Rebecca's nature to remain in low spirits for long. She was in any case of a pragmatic outlook and recognised that moping would not bring Hugo back to England. And even if he did return, would it make any difference? Might it not be a greater torture to have him close at hand and be treated only as a friend? Instead she took to considering her other friendships and taking comfort in them. When the time came for her to return to Lincolnshire, as she assuredly must, she would be surrounded by those who loved her, and now there was a niece to cherish also. This would be her future.

Lady Sawcroft did her utmost to introduce her protégée to the most eligible unmarried men of her acquaintance. Certainly it was gratifying to see her sought after, though it pleased her too that Rebecca wasn't above enjoying the company of those young ladies with whom she came into contact. One such girl was the granddaughter of a distant cousin of Matilda. The link was tenuous and, had they not been up to scratch, Lady Sawcroft would certainly have been more than capable of cutting the connection. She saw no reason to do so. Lydia Waddesdon had brought Emily to London at the request of her widowed son, who had hired a fine house for them and bestowed upon his daughter and her grandmother sufficient funds to enable them to enjoy such delights of the capital as were deemed appropriate. All that was lacking was the means of introducing Emily into circles unknown to herself, and it was thus that she applied to Matilda in much the same way as Elizabeth had on Becca's behalf.

"You will understand, my dear cousin, that it is my son's wish to see the child suitably established. He has become something of a recluse since his wife's passing and, well, not to put too fine a point on it, but I had to badger him into letting me bring the girl to town."

"Could you not have introduced her into Bath society?" asked Lady Sawcroft.

Lydia sat back and folded her hands in her lap, her head on one side and her expression quizzical.

Lady Sawcroft immediately demanded an answer to her question. "Come along, now. The truth, if you please."

"So be it. I do not live with my son. He resides in the middle of nowhere, and my poor Emily has been left with only her governess for company. Arthur does not go out, nor does he entertain. I leave you to imagine what sort of a life that is for a young lady. You are right that I live in Bath, but I could not resist the opportunity to come to London and bring my granddaughter with me." Here a somewhat gleeful expression passed across her features, taking years off her age and reminding Matilda of the reports in her salad days of what a mischievous girl her cousin had been. No stranger to devilry herself, she could comprehend exactly the motives behind Lydia's actions.

"I see. So you coerced him into sending you here."

"A strong word, my dear Matilda. Let us just say that I reminded him his daughter is already twenty years of age and must, if action is not taken soon, be left on the shelf and that he would be the one to blame for having made no push to see her suitably settled."

"And how did you persuade him that London would be preferable to Bath?"

Lydia picked up her fan and opened it, covering her face so that only her eyes could be seen. Laughing eyes, full of fun. "Money is no object. Once I had, as you say, persuaded him, he left all in my hands. I am not getting any younger. I cannot remember how long it has been since I last visited town. There isn't a soul I don't know in Bath. I fancied a change. I am determined to see Emily established, but I saw no reason why I should not enjoy myself at the same time."

Matilda laughed aloud. "Well, Lydia, you have certainly come to the right place. Now, tell me, what is it you would have me do for the girl?"

"A few introductions should do it. She is a pretty thing but not too forward. She will not offend mamas with daughters to turn off. And if they have sons too, well, my granddaughter is an heiress. I make no doubt her fortune will attract people to her as well. It will be my duty to separate the toadeaters from those who might have a genuine feeling for her. A fine line to walk, but I do not doubt my ability to do so."

Lady Sawcroft didn't doubt it either but felt compelled to add, "There are some unscrupulous men, unsuitable men, who might worm their way into the girl's affections."

"So would it be wherever I took her."

"You will not be offended if I offer you a word of advice?"

"Of course not."

"Don't let it be known that she is wealthy. If she is as personable as you suggest, she will succeed on her own merits." Matilda watched as her words took effect.

"I see. Yes, perhaps you are right."

"Where is she now, by the way?"

"I left her at home, writing a letter to her father. Our conversation could not have been so open had she been with me."

"You are a shrewd woman, Lydia. Very well. I will do what I can. It so happens that I am organising a few events for a young friend of mine. I see no reason why your Emily should not be included. None at all."

And so began a friendship between Rebecca and Emily which gave comfort and courage to both.

CHAPTER SEVEN

Hugo made his way to the Château du Berge by easy stages, giving him plenty of time to consider his position. It was not, in his opinion, a happy one. Countless were the times he re-read his mother's letters to Pierre. But most of all he thought of Rebecca, for she filled his dreams as well as many of his daylight hours.

When he had left the château a few months ago, some of the renovation work had been completed, but there was still much to be done. Even if he had not uncovered new evidence in England, he would have been obliged to return to the Loire soon enough. It was only his love for his friend's sister that had kept him so long away. His family home had been built by his ancestors, a blend of traditional medieval forms and classic Renaissance structures. So lavish was it that it had come as a considerable shock to him when he had first seen it upon returning to France after his uncle's death. He had no memories of his early childhood, and so he had never been able to picture the château. It was fortunate indeed that the building remained intact, for there had been much looting.

"So you see, there is nothing left to throw light upon what might have been here before," he said to his valet, throwing his arms wide to emphasise his point when all had been unpacked and they were at leisure to explore their surroundings. Hugo chose to reveal each room to Henri himself, a task that would certainly take more than a day.

"When you engaged me in Paris, Monsieur le Comte, I had no idea I would be working for one with such a history. It was not unknown, forgive me, for those who had fallen upon hard times to adopt a title which did not belong to them. It seems I must ask for an increase in my wage."

Hugo was not without a sense of humour. When last he had returned home he had left his man behind, suffering as he was from a broken arm sustained in defence of his master when some ne'er-do-well had knocked upon the door of his chambers. Henri had not seen the château and his master had told him little about it, other than mentioning that he had a property in the Loire Valley.

"I was in fact considering a reduction. You may judge for yourself what sums might be required to put such a place in order. I may not be able to pay you even a small sum."

"That would be a shame indeed, monsieur, for it would mean I may not be able to dress you at all." The relationship between the two men was an unconventional one but, apart from Brew, Hugo had no truly close friends, not any in whom he would be comfortable bestowing his confidence. He trusted Henri implicitly. "There are no portraits, monsieur? No papers?"

"The only papers I have are those left to me by my uncle. I cannot say I have turned this place upside down because that would take a lifetime, but I have searched in what I would consider to be the obvious places. Nothing!"

His mouth turned down and Henri, familiar with his moods, sought to encourage him.

"Then we will search in the not so obvious places."

"You wish to help me?"

"Of course."

The smile returned.

"I am going out today, Henri," Hugo informed his valet two days later. "It may be that I will be away overnight, I am not sure. In any case, I shall not need you. Make yourself useful in whatever way you see fit. I have told the builders you are in charge in my absence. That raised an eyebrow or two, I can tell you."

Henri, though a gentleman's gentleman by profession, was not of the dignified sort personified by some of his counterparts. He'd had many incarnations before his current work and was willing to turn his hand to whatever Hugo demanded of him. He would be prepared to sustain more than merely a broken arm in his defence, for the comte had rescued him from almost certain death on the streets of Paris. It was how they had met, Hugo warding off three assailants and helping him back to his own nearby lodgings.

"And am I permitted to continue searching for evidence of your family?"

"Not only permitted but I implore you to do so. And if you find anything, perhaps I shall pay your wages after all." With that, he mounted his horse and waved a cheery *adieu*. He wasn't as light-hearted as he appeared, though. More he was filled with apprehension, for this day might prove to be momentous or it might be just another disappointment. His route to Sully-sur-Loire was straightforward enough and he rode at a steady pace, taking his time to get to know the gelding that he had purchased since his arrival. He didn't want to tire him out either, should it prove necessary to return that same day. Sully-sur-Loire was a small village, a scattering of houses on either side of the road. What lay behind and beyond he couldn't see. He dismounted and led his horse to a water trough, unsure of how to proceed. In the end he just rapped on the door of the next property he came to.

"*Bonjour. Je cherche* Anne-Marie."

It was little enough information, with no surname, and he wasn't surprised when the owner denied all knowledge of her. "But I am new to the village. Perhaps another will know."

His heart had plummeted but now lurched up into his throat once more. He bowed and moved on. Nobody came to the door of the next house, but at the third he received the answer he'd been hoping for. Sort of.

"Anne-Marie? Which one?"

"Which one?"

"*Mais oui.* Anne-Marie Laurent ou Anne-Marie Bernard?"

Hugo of course had no idea. "There are two?"

"It is not an unusual name."

The woman, middle-aged and evidently enjoying herself, leaned against the doorframe and waited. Hugo didn't want to impart too much information, but he would obviously have to offer more than he had so far. He informed his hostess that the person he searched for might be anything between forty and fifty years of age.

"Then it is of Anne-Marie Bernard that you speak, for the other is but seven years old."

He wanted to stamp his foot in frustration but instead laid a smile upon his face and asked, "Perhaps you could direct me to where she lives?"

The woman made a gesture with her head. "In the cemetery. She passed away three years since."

Hugo was devastated. Had he come all this way for nothing?

"She leaves a daughter, though, and a sister."

He had begun to move away, but the words halted him in his tracks. Of the sister he knew nothing. But the daughter — could it be Juliette?

"And do they live here still, her family?"

"Why would they not? One house from the end on the other side of the road. There is a climbing rose growing over the porch. You cannot miss it."

And miss it he didn't. He was, however, doomed to disappointment. No-one responded to his rap on the door and on his third attempt, an old man who was digging in the garden of the house next door said, "You may knock as many times as you like, but you won't get an answer. Gone, they are, a week or two since."

Hugo's heart sank to his boots and he realised he was shaking. "Gone? How so?"

"No good you asking me. I'm not in their confidence. Just said one day that they were off and would see me in a month."

From despair came relief. He had thought them gone forever, and with no clue as to how to track them down he had believed he'd been brought to *point non plus*. Hope was renewed and he thanked the man warmly and took his leave. For a moment he considered writing a note and pushing it under the door, but what could he say? And in any case, these were peasant homes and it was possible their occupants might be unable to read. Is this where his sister lived? He'd felt no connection but, standing at a gate in front of an empty house, why would he? He wondered how loose was the expression 'in a month'. He would return then and hope to find that the occupants had come back. In the meantime, there was much to do at the château. More than sufficient to occupy him for many months. Certainly he would not be idle.

As he rode slowly back, his thoughts turned to Rebecca. She would not be idle, for sure. Had she returned to London? Had another won her heart? Useless to torture himself, but he resolved to write to Brew. He had promised to keep him informed of his progress and, when his friend replied, he might that way gain some knowledge of what he had come to regard as his lost love.

"I fear your journey did not meet with the hoped for success, monsieur," Henri remarked when his master returned so swiftly.

"It was not what I'd wished for, but I do not despair. The name I carried with me was not unknown, though its owner is deceased these three years. However, I was informed of a daughter. Juliette, do you think? Sadly, whether it be my sister or no, she was away from home with a companion, I know not whom, and is not expected to return for some weeks. But there is promise. Of a certainty there is promise. I shall return. In the meantime, there is much to do here. I presume nothing momentous has happened in the short time I was absent?"

Henri smirked. "I wouldn't say that, exactly. I was in the west wing for no other reason than the necessity of beginning my search somewhere. I was not optimistic, you understand."

Hugo could barely contain his impatience. "*Alors*, you found something?"

"There is a stone stairway carved where the wall is of such a thickness that you would imagine it would lend itself to hiding a secret, and for this very reason it is the last place one would look."

"*Mais pourquoi?*"

"Too obvious. But me, I am of a curious nature and I did look. On a landing there is a door. I opened it. Merely a cupboard. A strange place to put a cupboard, I thought, so out of the way. The shelves were but inches deep. Of what use might it be?"

"Come on, man, show me," Hugo said, not even bothering to change out of his riding clothes and heading off at a run. He could barely contain his excitement. Henri showed him where he had run his fingers under the bottom shelf and had found a catch in the back corner. The whole cupboard swung outwards, away from them, to reveal more stone steps leading downwards.

"Have a care, monsieur, it is slippery."

It was unlit, but Henri had brought some tallow candles in readiness and Hugo led the way. There was no stirring in the air and the flame held steady until they reached a small chamber that had been carved out of the wall.

"You have been busy in my absence, have you not?" Even in the subdued lighting, Hugo's eyes could be seen to be glowing. There was room only for two small chairs and a table. Sconces on the wall showed that it had been prepared in readiness for a long stay. Shelves were carved along the whole of one wall and two were deep enough for a person to lie full length if need be. The upper shelves, shallower, held some paraphernalia that could have proved to be useful under certain circumstances. As Hugo felt his way along, he was convinced one of the blocks of stone moved under his hand. Upon further investigation he found it could be pulled out and, hidden behind it, were two strongboxes. He carefully lifted both down and put them on the table.

"I touched nothing, monsieur. I did not think it was my place."

"I am almost frightened to look." The boxes were not locked. Why would they be, when they'd been so carefully hidden away? Hugo opened first one and then the other. Both contained documents. "We will carry them back to somewhere more comfortable, for this is not going to be the task of a few moments. Well done, man!"

Henri told him that he'd been outside and had examined the building from the ground. Such was the configuration that there was no clue as to what the wall held hidden. "I could find no access from outside nor exit from within, but of course I had barely time to discover what I did before your return. I had come looking for some candles to facilitate the search when you came back."

Few of the many rooms were yet fit for habitation, but one that Hugo had set aside for personal use during his previous visit was reasonably comfortable, having since been decorated although as yet sparsely equipped. Henri left his master sitting at the desk, some bookshelves being the only other furniture, which left the space feeling at present cold and unwelcoming. Hugo didn't notice. Heat came from within as he leaned back in his chair, staring at the two boxes. Finally, he leaned forward and pulled one towards him. The first document had been written by his father. There could be no doubt, because it began *Je suis le Comte du Berge*. He got no further, the pages trembling in his unsteady hands. Never before had Hugo consciously held anything his father had touched before him. He imagined a tingling sensation in his fingers, then steadied himself and began to read.

His father had written of his fear for his family. Of the atrocities that were happening all around them. Of the terror that prevented him from sleeping in case soldiers should come for them during the night. He begged that whoever should find this box would seek out his son in England. He gave Pierre's name but no address. It would seem the document had been written before Hugo's uncle had reached his destination with his young charge, or he surely would have given his direction.

It stated further that much of the comte's wealth had travelled with his brother but that what remained might be found in the box from which this letter had been taken. Hugo read the final lines:

If you are reading this and I am not here to tell the tale, I will certainly have perished. I pray my wife and baby daughter survive. Take care of them, if you will, and have compassion. They are not to be blamed for this crazy world in which we live.

Hugo shivered. A rectangle of red velvet covered the remainder of the contents of the box and he pulled it away. One by one, he removed the jewels. Diamonds. Rubies. All manner of gems in exquisite settings. The one that most affected him, though, was a ring. His father's signet ring. Slowly, savouring the moment, he slid it onto his finger.

Returning the treasure and moving the first box to one side, Hugo pulled the second towards him. It was smaller than the other and contained only a few letters. He recognised the hand immediately. It was his mother's, and it was evident from the contents that it had been written some time after that of his father.

I am in despair. It is weeks now since Anne-Marie took Juliette away and I carry my guilt every moment, not on her account, because there is no doubt that her only hope of survival was to be removed from me. No, I carry a dark secret in my breast, and I pray that when my time comes God will forgive me.

Jacques sacrificed himself on my behalf. We knew the soldiers were coming. He insisted I hide here, and told me he would inform them that he had sent me and my children away. He has been gone three days now, and every time I hear a noise I fear the enemy has returned and I come to my hole to hide. There has been much activity in the surrounding area. They are searching everywhere. I have written two more letters to Pierre, but I have no recollection of his direction. These English words tie my tongue, and in any case I have no means of sending them now. They are in my box. I will die here and I will never again be able to tell him how much I loved him. Or hold my son. Or my daughter.

There was some smudging where no doubt his mother's tears had fallen onto the page.

Only one thing is to my credit, which is that I did not tell Jacques of my perfidy. He was a good man and did not deserve what happened, but at least he died believing his wife to be faithful. But wait. There are people in the château. They are come. Heaven help me, they are come. My courage fails. Adieu, sweet life, adieu.

Hugo shed tears of his own. He had no reproof for his mother. One could not choose where one lost one's heart, he of all people knew that. He read her letters to Pierre, only in case they might shed more light. They did not. They were but an outpouring of her love. He tried not to imagine what had happened when she'd said that last *adieu*. Had they dragged her from her hiding place, or had she been executed on the spot? She'd had time only to return her box to its hiding place before she'd been discovered, of that he was sure, for it would not otherwise have been there. How she'd had the strength to move the block of stone, he could not know. Desperation, perhaps. Hugo sat staring ahead, seeing nothing.

A while later came a discreet knock on the door, and Henri came in without waiting to be bidden to enter. "It grows late, monsieur, and your dinner awaits." Seeing his master's face, he almost wished that he had not revealed the hidden chamber, but Hugo shook off his reverie and rose to his feet.

"You are right. I had lost all sense of time. Lead me to it, though at the moment a drink would be preferable to food."

"You shall have both, sir."

CHAPTER EIGHT

Lady Sawcroft would never have admitted that with Louisa at Merivale she was feeling a measure of loneliness, but the timing of Lydia Waddesdon's visit to town could not have been more fortuitous. Consideration of any pretension was set aside in her delight at finding one with a sense of humour to match her own. And the woman was realistic, too. She had a goal and Matilda had no doubt she would stick to it. It was important, though, to keep Emily's expectations concealed, or every fortune hunter in London would be after her.

Having two young women to promote was proving to be far less arduous that might have been imagined for ladies who were advanced in years.

"You can see, can you not, Lydia, how Emily and Miss Ware complement each other? Neither your granddaughter, with her dark brown eyes and even darker brown hair, nor Rebecca, with her blonde curls and blue eyes, is overshadowed by the other. More, I believe the differences between them only enhance their appearance."

"I agree, and though Miss Ware has a strong personality which I know will appeal to many gentlemen, my Emily has a shyness about her that will bring out a protective instinct in others. I have little doubt that the impact of the two together will carry more weight than were they to appear separately."

"To be sure, we have only to put them in the way of the right people and we may leave it to them to do the rest. Both are fully aware of what is expected of them. You will forgive me if I sound scheming, but it is the way of the world that marriage is the only occupation for young women of their status."

"And that, my dear Matilda, is why I have brought Emily to London and applied to you for assistance. Fate has smiled upon my granddaughter, and she need never want for anything, but I would rather give her the opportunity to meet gentlemen with that certain touch of something about them than that she settle for one who cares only for his lands and his horses."

"And I shall be as frank with you, Lydia. Rebecca has no fortune to recommend her, but she is a beautiful and accomplished young woman with no reason to blush for her lineage. What she needs is a gentleman of sufficient wealth and standing who mixes in all the right circles."

And so they plotted. Both women, having in their own minds satisfactorily disposed of their charges, sat back in the carriage which was now stationary and waited for the return of the girls who, along with Elizabeth, were strolling in the park, with no clue that their futures were being mapped out for them. It was Mrs Ware who first spotted Lady Sawcroft's conveyance and said she was thankful, since her boots were pinching and she would be happy to have the opportunity to give her feet a rest. "Such a disappointment, for the leather is so soft and they seemed perfect to me. It was only when I began to walk in them that I realised my error."

Her daughter laughed, though sympathetically. "Poor Mama. You know you only bought them because there were so pretty. Perhaps you may return them to be stretched or, if not, you could merely wear them about the house where you may enjoy their beauty without suffering discomfort."

"You are right — it would be such a pity to have to dispose of them. And here we are, and with the steps already let down. I shall get in first."

"Would you mind if Emily and I continued without you? It is such a lovely day that it seems a shame to curtail the pleasure, and we have our maids in attendance to safeguard our reputations."

Miss Waddesdon, having developed a deep admiration for Rebecca, was only too ready to add her pleas. Elizabeth, who had by this time climbed into the carriage, leaned forward, acquiescing but urging them to be sure to return to their respective homes in time to prepare for the ball that they were all to attend later. Emily could speak of little but the forthcoming evening, the first of such she was to attend since her arrival. One or two gentlemen who were unknown to them, delighted at finding seemingly unattended ladies in the park, attempted to engage them in conversation. They came to realise their mistake when Rebecca raised a haughty eyebrow, and the proximity of their maids soon put paid to any pretension. And then Becca spotted Amabel and Gil coming towards them.

"How lovely to see you, ladies," Gil greeted. "You will not object if we turn about and join you?"

"Of course not, Gil. We have been so busy I've hardly had a chance to see you since you arrived. Do you go to the Byfleets' ball tonight?"

"We do, and Amabel here is looking forward to it immensely, are you not, my dear? Particularly as she has now had the opportunity to have a few alterations made to her gown."

"And I have some new gloves and slippers, purchased at a delightful emporium, Becca," added Amabel. "But you will know of it, of course, since we went there together with Lady Sawcroft last year."

"Oh yes, I know the one you refer to. It has become a favourite of mine." Becca turned to Gil, unable to resist teasing him. "And will you be dazzling us with some fine, not to say colourful attire?"

"You would expect nothing less of me, surely."

They carried on in this manner for a while and, in the safety of Mr Carstairs' company, stopped several times to speak with one or other of his friends whom they met along the way. All this gentle banter succeeded in putting the usually shy Emily at her ease and made Rebecca glad she had suggested they continue their walk. When they eventually parted company, it was in anticipation of an enjoyable evening to come.

Elizabeth Ware entered her daughter's bedchamber to find her sitting in front of a dresser regarding her image in the glass that stood upon it. Becca's maid, Alice, had just finished arranging her hair, which was for the most part caught up with pins but from which two or three dark blonde ringlets had been allowed to fall on either side of her face. Catching sight of her mother in the mirror, Becca dismissed the abigail and started to rise, but Elizabeth's hands upon her shoulders urged her to remain where she was.

"The girl has a way with your hair for sure. You are looking delightful, my child." Two pairs of blue eyes met in the glass, and Elizabeth continued, "You are looking troubled. Surely you are not nervous?"

Becca swivelled round to face her and grasped her hands. "Of the ball? No, for I love the music and the dancing, meeting new people, and oh, everything about it. If I am troubled, it is because I have been less than honest with you."

Elizabeth moved away and, smoothing the folds of her own ballgown, sat carefully on the edge of the bed. "Is it something you wish to discuss now, before we go?"

"I believe I would be more comfortable, yes." And once Becca began to bare her soul, the words fell from her lips and the whole tale was revealed. She told of how much she had liked Hugo before she'd ever fallen in love with him. She confided that he was a man to whom she felt she could say anything — although she could not tell him of her feelings, of course — and their time at Merivale had only augmented how she felt, thrown together as they were.

"I had suspected as much after something you wrote to me. And does he return your regard?" asked Elizabeth.

"I hoped so. I thought so. But he never went beyond what was conventional, and though there was something in his demeanour that convinced me he felt as I did, he never spoke a word of it. And now he has returned to France, and I don't know if I will ever see him again."

She managed to control the break in her voice, but Elizabeth felt something heavy in her breast. "My poor girl. After what you endured last year, fate has been cruel indeed to deal you another blow."

Becca went to her mother, sat beside her and turned a trembling smile upon her. "No, Mama, you misunderstand. Last year was a tragedy, but now I have found a love that will endure forever — on my side, anyway. I am grateful for the time I had with Hugo, but I have found the strength to move on. I will always cherish those days in Kent as the happiest of my life, but it's time to start again. I have observed that in real life it is preferable, perhaps, to look for mutual respect and contentment in one's partner rather than have an expectation of strong emotions which cannot possibly be sustained." Her mother wept inwardly to hear her daughter speak so, but Rebecca smiled again. "Now that I have unburdened myself, I feel so much better. Truly, I am looking forward to what is to come, but I could not proceed without confiding in you, my best of mothers."

"Well, stand up then, and let me look at you properly. We chose well, I think. Jonquil suits you admirably. Which reminds me — wait here a moment, if you will," Elizabeth said and went tripping out of the room. She was back a moment later, carrying a small box. "I had meant to bring this with me before," she added, placing it on the dresser and removing a single row of pearls. "These will be perfect. Your neck is beautiful, and you need something not to hide but to enhance it. There. Don't you agree?"

Elizabeth's taste was faultless, and when they left for the ball a short while later, she knew her daughter was looking outstandingly beautiful. Had she been merely demonstrating her bravery earlier, or was she truly ready to put the past behind her and look to the future? Only time would tell.

Several hours later, Elizabeth had to admit she didn't know whether Rebecca had spoken the truth or not, but if she had any regrets, she was keeping them close. In fact, her daughter was able to reply honestly when Emily asked if she was not having a wonderful time.

"I think it a splendid evening, and I'm so happy that your first such experience has proved to be such a pleasant one."

"I have taken my lead from you and, forgive me, followed your example," said Emily. "You have a way of looking directly at whomsoever you are speaking to without in any way putting yourself forward. Grandmamma has been entreating me not to shrink within myself, and I didn't understand what she meant until I had the chance to observe you. I hope you don't mind. After an hour or so I found I was able, when introduced to someone new, to do the same. Not only did it prevent me from appearing as a gawky schoolgirl, but it also gave me the courage in some part to overcome my shyness. I would never have believed I could enjoy myself so much."

Rebecca too was surprised at what a pleasant time she was having. Her earlier words to her mother had been sincere enough, but putting her resolve into action had proved to be easier by far than she'd anticipated. There had been two dances for which her hand had not been solicited, but as she was engaged in conversation all the while she barely noticed. Amabel had advised her that when they'd returned from their walk earlier in the day, it was to find a letter from her mother, who was able to inform her that Harriet was very nearly fully recovered. "She hopes that Gil and I will be able to visit Merivale before long, for she tells me, Becca, that you and I have the most beautiful niece."

"You will have no argument from me on that score. Nancy is the sweetest thing. Do you go then to Kent?"

Amabel laughed. "I think Mama would not forgive me, were I to fail her. But here is Gil and with him Mr Saltaire, whom you met this morning in the park."

"Yes, I remember. A friend from his university days, I believe."

Gil bore his wife off to dance and when Robert Saltaire invited Becca to do the same, she demurred and said, if he didn't mind, she would prefer to sit this one out and talk instead. He was surprised by her unusual manner but was delighted to have the opportunity of furthering his acquaintance with her, and when it was time to go down to supper he asked if he might escort her. Becca looked round for

Emily, for she felt responsible for her, but she spotted her with Lady Sawcroft and Lydia Waddesdon. Thus it was without qualms that she accepted the invitation, happy to be in the company of one with whom it was so easy to converse.

The next day brought a steady stream of morning callers to Grosvenor Square. Although the Wares, already established in town, were accustomed to receiving visitors, their number increased following the Byfleet ball, where many new acquaintances had been struck up. Robert Saltaire was one of them, and he contrived to have only a few moments with Rebecca before another joined them, and then another, making private conversation impossible. He managed only to say on leaving that he hoped to see her in the park the next day. She was surprised, therefore, to receive a note from him an hour later, inviting her to drive with him instead and saying that his groom would wait for a reply.

"What do you think, Mama? Would it be proper for me to go?"

"Mr Saltaire would not, I am sure, seek to compromise you in any way. Doubtless he will have his tiger up behind him, and if he is driving you will be on view the whole time." Elizabeth could see she was still hesitating. "What troubles you? Ah, you are thinking of Dorian Fletcher, are you not?"

"I am. After all, this is hardly dissimilar, accompanying a gentleman in his carriage."

"The circumstances may be alike, but the men in question are not. In any case, you are a little more up to scratch this year and will not be taken in by silky comments. Not that I believe Mr Saltaire would be guilty or even capable of such."

"No, he has a serious turn of mind which I find refreshing."

"Then I see no reason not to accept his invitation. It will give me an opportunity also to write to your father, who must be wondering what has become of us. I haven't written for several days, and I promised I would keep him advised of what's toward."

Rebecca laughed and her mother responded with a wide smile.

"I think Papa will not have given us a second thought, but yes, I will go tomorrow. Now, I must not keep the groom waiting any longer." She dashed off a quick reply before asking her mother if there was anything she wished to do for the rest of the afternoon.

"There is hardly time if we are to join Lady Sawcroft at the theatre this evening. She is being very kind to us, is she not?"

"Indeed she is, but I make no doubt she is enjoying herself immensely. She is not one to sit idly at home with her needlepoint while others are out taking pleasure in all that is on offer. Lady Sawcroft would always, I surmise, be one who leads, rather than one who follows. She has as much energy as I do, and I am but half her age."

"You are right. Even having a simple conversation with her leaves me breathless. All in all, though, a very agreeable woman."

"She seems also to be taking a delight in promoting the fortunes of Emily Waddesdon, though they are but loosely connected. A generous spirit, to be sure."

Mother and daughter spent the next little while in silent companionship, tea being the only interruption, each occupied with a book borrowed from Hookham's Library, until it was time to get changed for the evening.

Other guests who attended Lady Sawcroft's box at the theatre were Lydia Waddesdon and her granddaughter, Mr and

Mrs Carstairs and two gentlemen whom Rebecca was certain had been invited for the express purpose of becoming acquainted with herself and Emily. One was another university friend of Gil's who had but recently arrived in town, and the other was a terrified-looking young man, who was the son of an old friend of Lady Sawcroft. He called her Aunt Matilda but was no relation. During the first interval he was for a few minutes alone with Becca and at once confided in her, "The old lady makes me quake in my boots, Miss Ware. It has ever been the same. I have known her since I was in leading strings. I think it's to do with the way she always emphasises the first syllable of my name. Henry, she says, and makes it sound like a reprimand."

Becca was hugely entertained by him. Away from Matilda, it was to be found that Henry Holland was blessed with a delicious sense of humour and she was delighted he formed one of the party. With Amabel and Gil she was always at ease. Rebecca had no opportunity for conversation with the other man, aside from the initial introduction. He was quite obviously bent on entertaining Emily Waddesdon and, by the animated look on her face, was succeeding very well.

"It's good to see Mr Radcliff putting Emily at her ease, Gil. All this is very new to her, and I know she won't mind me telling you she is a trifle shy."

"Rufus? Yes, he always had a way with the ladies even when we were at Oxford. I haven't seen him for years, as it so happens, but I ran across him at White's the other day. I believe he's been living abroad. Anyway, when Lady Sawcroft asked me if I had any single male friends she could invite this evening — you know what she's like — I thought of him, Robert Saltaire already being engaged."

"She is a determined matchmaker, is she not?" Becca said, smiling back at him. "And there's the bell. We must take our places again for the next act."

The box was filled with visitors again in the next interval and Robert Saltaire, who was a guest elsewhere, stopped by only for long enough to thank Rebecca for accepting his invitation and to say how much he was looking forward to driving her the following day. "I shall not see you again this evening, as I do not enjoy the farce. My mind is of a more serious turn, which I suspect makes me a bit of a dull dog. Until tomorrow then, Miss Ware."

The following day, Robert Saltaire was on time and Rebecca was ready.

"You are a woman full of surprises, Miss Ware. I had anticipated asking my groom to walk the horses for at least ten minutes."

"But that would have been rude, would it not?"

"Not so much rude as expected of your fair sex."

"Well, you will not find me so. They are a fine pair," she said, nodding at the bays as he handed her up into the carriage.

"You are a judge?"

She smiled. There was no undertone to his question, as though a woman could not be expected to appreciate good cattle when she saw them; it seemed more that he was interested. "Not especially, but I like to think I can differentiate between bone-setters and those with a bit of something about them. Where are you taking me, Mr Saltaire?"

"I had thought we might go to the park, though I suspect I shall be obliged to draw rein several times if those of your friends who are walking wish to wave us down."

"If they do, sir, we shall ignore them. I should like the opportunity to have a proper conversation with you without constant interruption."

He made her laugh then by saying that he would in that case run down anyone who had the temerity to stand in the way of the carriage. They had by this time reached the park and he turned in, negotiating the gates with ease, and proceeded at a trot before slowing his horses to a walk so that they might converse more easily.

"I understand you have known Gil Carstairs since your Oxford days," said Becca. "You must know he is a neighbour of mine and we have lived in each other's pockets our whole lives. You are not alike, you and he."

Again an appreciative smile. "Hardly. I have neither the figure nor the inclination to adorn my person with any of the outrageously attention-seeking attire he adopts. So are our characters different, but I am happy to say that ours is a friendship that has endured despite — or maybe because of — our not meeting often. My home is in an altogether different part of the country, and I believe neither of us spend much of the year in London."

Rebecca found she was enjoying herself quite as much as she had anticipated and was glad he appreciated the joke when she said, "And after you left the theatre yesterday, I can tell you no-one took more pleasure in the farce than Gil. Even more so than Amabel. No, you are not alike, that is certain."

Robert smiled. "I am wondering, Miss Ware, how long you might be remaining in town," he said, turning the subject.

"For a few more weeks, I believe. I'm not sure if my mother plans to return to Kent, where my brother and sister-in-law are staying for the time being, at Harriet's old home. It may be that I will go with her, or I might remain. Lady Sawcroft has offered to take me in if I do. You may know that the major and his wife live close by us in Lincolnshire, so Mama may wait until we return home to see them again."

"Have you had the opportunity yet to visit Ranelagh? I understand the Chinese pavilion is exceptional. It is also my belief that there is to be a balloon ascension at Vauxhall next month. Perhaps I may be permitted to escort you to one or the other."

"I should be delighted but, since I haven't yet been to either, I must leave it to you to choose, sir."

"Both, then," which comment caused the horses to fall into a trot as Rebecca and Robert broke into laughter. He brought his team under control again and apologised.

"No, don't. It's good to see you are not perfect."

"What! Heaven forfend."

Becca had a most enjoyable time. Her host was neither lover-like nor away in the clouds but entertained her hugely. Satisfied that it was an attraction of minds, she was able to relax completely in his company and even to feel a trifle vexed when they were waved down by Amabel and Gil, who were walking in the park.

"I can't very well run them over, you know," said Robert, pulling up. He raised his voice and remarked, "Good morning. Your servant, Mrs Carstairs. Mr Carstairs. We were just talking about you."

"Amabel, that bonnet becomes you very well. I'm so glad you chose that and not the other," Becca said, referring to a recent shopping expedition they had enjoyed together. "Why, it even perfectly matches your husband's coat," which made all four laugh, since it was of a bold green.

"You must allow me my affectations, Becca," Gil replied. "My clothes are my only extravagance."

"Most certainly I do. Just consider what pleasure you give the rest of us, never knowing what new delights you will have adopted for our gratification the next time we see you."

Robert then excused them, remarking with good humour that even though Gil's sartorial elegance was an interesting subject for discussion, he must not keep his horses standing longer. He then drove Rebecca home, asking before he left if he might procure tickets for Ranelagh Gardens for the following week.

"I shall look forward to it, and will see also if I can procure a copy of that book you recommended."

Becca's step was lighter as she tripped up the steps and into the house. It wasn't long since she would have been hard put to believe she might have taken so much pleasure in such an outing. For a moment a cloud passed across her features as she thought of Hugo, and her mother, who looked up as she entered the room, asked if she had not enjoyed herself.

"Why, yes, Mama, I have had a delightful time. Mr Saltaire is an interesting man and we talked of all manner of things. And then we stopped for a while to talk to Amabel and Gil. And you would not have believed the colour of Gil's coat! You must remember the bonnet Amabel purchased the other day. It was of an identical hue."

"Would I not indeed? You must remember I have known Gil all his life. Nothing he chooses to wear would astonish me, unless of course it was something subdued, more in the style of your brother."

Elizabeth had more sense than to ask her daughter if she hoped to see Robert again, but she was relieved to observe a lifting of her mood. She could only guess at what had caused the frown and prayed it would appear less frequently as time went on.

CHAPTER NINE

Even losing himself in first one bottle of wine and then another could not rid Hugo's mind of the vision of his mother, waiting in terror for her own execution, and cowering in a chamber that was no longer a secret, never again to see the light of day. Eventually the faithful Henri half led, half carried him to his bedchamber. He awoke the next morning with his face as grey as the sky he could see through the window, for his valet had drawn the curtains aside. He had a headache that he knew would remain with him for the rest of the day. Henri knew better than to speak to him when he brought in his hot chocolate, but Hugo eased himself up into a sitting position and said with some effort, "I assume it is thanks to you that I slept in my bed last night and not slumped on the floor in the library. In the light of what I found in those boxes, I must tell you that any wish I had cherished died when I read what were surely my mother's last words. All my hope now lies in finding my sister but —" he grimaced as he swung his legs over the side and stood up — "as I cannot pursue that avenue for some weeks, we will concentrate on putting the château in order."

"It is your intention to remain here, then?"

"For the future? I do not know. But for the moment I can't leave it in its present condition. I owe that much to my ancestors and to the memory of my parents. For now, once I have breakfasted, I would ask you to meet me in the library, where there are complete plans which I asked to be drawn up when last I came. Together we will decide how to tackle the renovations — there are more than enough to keep me occupied until I can once more return to Sully-sur-Loire."

Two hours later, they were poring over the details not just of the château itself but also of the surrounding grounds.

"As we are fixed here for some considerable time, it will be necessary to engage more staff. I will ride over this afternoon to a neighbour whose acquaintance I made when last I came in the hope that he may give me the direction of a trustworthy steward. I had hoped to return to England for a while, but that is out of the question at the moment."

There was little Henri didn't know about his master, but he could only speculate on his feelings for Miss Ware, since Hugo had not confided in him. However, his intimate knowledge of the man was sufficient to convince him that there was something in the air, so to speak. He had left Merivale not in the high spirits to be expected when embarking on an adventure; it was more as if he'd left a part of himself behind. Was that why he'd hoped to return to England? Henri couldn't know. All he could do was devote himself to helping put his house in order and, more importantly, praying that he might find his sister alive and well.

Hugo was very busy for the next few days. He was fortunate in that his neighbour was able to offer the hoped-for introduction and that Monsieur Durant was able to begin work immediately, his previous employer having recently died with no heirs to inherit his property. It wasn't until a week later that Hugo finally sat down to write to Brew:

Cher Brew,

It is my sincere hope that your belle femme has returned to full health and that you are enjoying the new addition to your family. Do you remain at Merivale, or have you returned to London, or even Lincolnshire? I have decided to remain in France for a while, for reasons which I will now explain.

You will know that I had hoped to uncover information regarding the circumstances of my parents' demise and, if possible, to trace my sister. I can tell you now that there is no doubt both died within a few days of each other. As for Juliette, I have some news, though very little at the moment. I traced Anne-Marie — you will remember she was my mother's maid — to the village of Sully-sur-Loire, only to discover that she died three years ago. You may imagine my despair, to come so near and then... However, I was informed she had left behind a daughter and a sister. Could the daughter be my Juliette? I was directed to a cottage, but there was no-one home. A neighbour informed me the occupants were absent and not expected to return within the month, so I must now bide my time, a much easier thing to say than to do.

If it is indeed she, what will I find? She has been raised as a peasant girl, but if she is truly my flesh and blood I cannot just leave her to her fate, though I have no idea as yet what I might do. But I run ahead of myself. I have not even met her. It might not be she. I try not to think of that possibility, for I have pinned my hopes upon finding her. When you and I meet again — heaven knows when that will be — I will tell you more of my mother. The circumstances are too distressing for me to put them in a letter.

Do let me know how you get on and where I may find you — I presume my letter will be redirected, if you are no longer in Kent. Remember me to your mother and sister. I spent many happy hours with them, for which I will always be grateful. It is my hope that I will see them again when I return to England.

Hugo

In between overseeing the renovations at the château, Hugo occupied himself with visiting the various properties which were within his boundaries and still remained in his ownership.

It was evident that some of the tenants were in fear of any charges he might levy or that he would expect some payment for all the years they had managed their farms rent-free. He reassured each one, saying that what was in the past might best remain there but that his newly-appointed steward might strike up some arrangement which was fair and satisfactory to all. He took the mantle of landowner upon himself with unexpected ease and, because he had an air of authority but no arrogance about him, immediately endeared himself to his tenants.

In the end Hugo added an extra week to the four he had been given before returning to Sully-sur-Loire, dreading to find his quarry had not yet returned, or perhaps restraining himself for fear of what he might discover. He tied his horse's rein to a convenient post and, heart in mouth, approached the cottage once more. A young woman, close to him in age and even closer in countenance, appeared in the doorway. There could be no doubt. Near-black hair framed a face with cheekbones and a determined chin that matched his own, and eyes as dark as his looked questioningly, then wonderingly, at her caller.

"Monsieur?"

"Juliette?"

"*Oui*, that is my name, but we have not met. I would have remembered."

She spoke with a softly cultured voice that reflected nothing of the peasant he had been expecting. How could this be? Hugo was lost for words. How should he proceed? What should he say, for he had made no plan beyond this point? She sensed his confusion and stood aside, inviting him into her home. "Perhaps you had better come in, sir."

Inside was a single room with a kitchen area to one side, a crude table and some chairs. A door at the back was of the type one might find in a stable, and the top half was open to reveal a garden. Another opening in the right-hand wall was hung with a curtain and no doubt led to a sleeping area.

"Please sit down and, well, I can see from your face that you have some explaining to do." She'd clearly seen their resemblance as well.

"Perhaps it would be advisable for you to sit also, for I have no doubt that what I am about to tell you will come as a surprise."

Hugo got no further. A woman appeared in the gap at the back of the house, her head bent as she released the catch on the lower half and swung it open. She looked up and, upon seeing Hugo, she fell in a dead faint on the floor. Hugo jumped to his feet and both he and Juliette rushed over. He swept her up into his arms, though they were shaking violently.

"Through there," Juliette said. "Lay her on her bed." Hugo did so while his sister poured some water from a jug and followed him into the side room. "She has never done such a thing in all her life!" Juliette dipped a cloth into the water and wiped the woman's brow. She did not stir.

"Who is she?" Hugo asked bluntly.

"She is my aunt. But why should your appearance have brought on such a reaction? Who *are* you?"

"Have you not guessed?"

"There is a resemblance between us, I can see. My aunt has it also, as you will no doubt have observed. My father died soon after I was born. I never knew him, and my mother died three years ago. Are you saying that she…? That you are a bastard? Or that I am?"

But it hadn't taken Hugo long, even though his brain was in turmoil, to realise the truth. How, though, had it come about? It was evident that Juliette had no inkling that the woman she referred to as her aunt was in fact her mother. Was *their* mother. And now he had to break the news to her. But would that be fair to the woman lying in a swoon beside them?

"I think perhaps it would be best if we wait until your aunt has recovered, and we can discuss it together, the three of us."

It didn't take long. Even as he spoke there was a moan from the woman who lay beside them and she stirred, propping herself up on her elbow before sitting up sufficiently abruptly to cause her to raise a hand to her forehead.

"Hugo? *Hugo?*"

"*Oui*, Maman. *C'est moi*," he whispered gently.

Juliette looked from one to the other in wonder.

"I thought I'd never see you again," Isabelle gasped, reaching for his hands.

"And I thought you dead. The note you left hidden in the château... *They are come*, you wrote. I believed... Well, you may imagine what I believed. What is the truth of what happened that day?"

She began to weep pitifully, gulping air until her sobs subsided. Her children waited without a word. Eventually, composed and able to speak once more, the Comtesse du Berge said, "Juliette does not know. Come, let us sit at the table and I will explain all."

She looked in wonderment at her son, unable to believe what was happening. And still her daughter was in the dark. Completely calm now, she began to speak and as her story unfolded a profusion of emotions swept across her children's faces.

"When I wrote that note I thought my last moments had arrived, but it was not the enemy who had come for me. It was Anne-Marie's brothers whom I heard approaching. She knew where the hidey-hole was, you understand. They urged me to go with them, fearing for my safety. Your father had been taken a few days before, while I was hidden away," she said, looking at Hugo.

"I am aware. You said as much in your note."

"If you have read that through, you will know also of my feelings for Pierre."

"That much I knew already. You had corresponded with him after we had arrived safely in England. Upon his death, I found your letters hidden in a secret compartment in his desk."

A look of pain marred Isabelle's still beautiful features. "I could not hope he still lived. How long?"

"A few years ago, but it is only now I've been able to uncover any evidence. Believing you had perished, it is Juliette I came in search of."

Juliette jumped up, paced a moment and then sat down again. "You speak in riddles, both of you. Explain!"

"You are not my niece, *ma belle*. You are my daughter. This is your brother Hugo, Comte du Berge."

"What!"

"You were a mere babe in arms. Hugo had been sent to England in the company of his uncle, my husband's younger brother, but I was too ill to travel. We were convinced the soldiers would come for us, and Anne-Marie — she was my maid — offered to take you to her village and raise you as her own. It was, we thought, your only hope of survival."

"But then you too came to Sully-sur-Loire. Why did you not then claim me as your own?"

"You cannot understand the fear we lived in. Who knows what might have happened, had it been found out that I was of noble birth? We put it about that I was Anne-Marie's sister, newly returned from service to a lady of consequence. It explained my speech — so different, you will agree, from hers."

"Yes, I was told that story as a child."

"As was everyone else. And as you grew, I taught you the things you would have known had you been raised as befitted your birth. You learned to sew — you will agree that at least has been useful. You learned to read; you developed a love of poetry. All manner of things — though sadly we had no instrument for me to teach you to play. We had no choice, once the deception had begun, but to continue. We were considered a little odd, but with all accepting you as Anne-Marie's child no-one ever suspected the truth. That we look alike was never questioned, because I was thought to be her sister and features are not always shared by direct descendants."

There were a few moments of silence as Juliette tried to absorb all that had been said, and Hugo's eyes didn't waver from his mother's face. It was he who spoke next.

"And why did you not return to the château when the troubles were over?"

"I had not the means to do so. We are poor. It didn't occur to me that the boxes we had left, Jacques and I, might still be there. That I might find anything of value. When they came to fetch me I was effectively dragged away, so important was haste, and I had no thought of bringing them with me. To tell the truth, I had forgotten about them. But I had not forgotten about you, Hugo. I could only dream that one day you might find me."

"And Pierre? Is he my uncle? Or is he perhaps my father?" Juliette broke in, her whole history in tatters.

Isabelle lowered her eyes but brought them up to look steadily into those of her daughter. "In all honesty, I cannot tell you. You look like me, but the truth is that the resemblance between the brothers too was strong. Never doubt, though, that you were conceived in love. I loved them both, you see; think of me what you will."

"It is not for me to judge. To discover that you are my mother, and to find I have a brother, these are enough for me to deal with. So, what happens now?"

Hugo sat back in his chair and looked from one to the other. And then he laughed and laughed. Eventually he said, "I do not know. But I am so very happy. Before I came here today, I could only hope that I might find a sister. To discover that my mother too is alive, it is sufficient for one day, *n'est ce pas?*"

Hugo left soon after. There was no doubt both women had received a severe shock and, in the case of Juliette, perhaps not in a good way. He couldn't rid his mind of her comment as he took his leave.

"My whole life, it has been a lie then," she'd said, large brown eyes glistening with tears.

"Only for your protection, Juliette, and for our mother's also," he'd answered. "Be brave. I shall come and see you again tomorrow. Be assured I will take care of you."

But he knew she must fear the future. What did she know of his world? She may have been poor, but she was contented. He could only be thankful that her gaze followed him as he mounted his horse and rode away. She was still looking when he glanced over his shoulder to wave *adieu*. At least she hadn't turned away abruptly and closed the door on him in undue haste. He would have given much to have heard what was said after he left, but this was a conversation they needed to have, just the two of them.

As he trotted home he found himself thinking about what might happen next. The château was not yet fit for habitation, not for two women; they would be happier for a while in their cottage. With that thought, he broke into a canter, the wind in his face, and for a short time he left the world to take care of itself.

Henri was waiting for him, anxious for news, but he had only to see his master's bearing to know that his mission had been successful. "You found her?"

"*Bien sûr*, for I am smiling, as you can see. But there is more. So much more."

"Tell me, then."

Hugo sat down and gestured to Henri to do the same. With their shared history, there was little evidence of the relationship of employee and valet. They were friends; they had been through too much together to be otherwise. The comte has taken a bottle and two glasses from a dresser which stood against the wall, opposite the middle of three windows. He poured a drink for each of them, sat back, threw one leg across the other and explained all that had occurred.

"And what will you do now?" gasped Henri. "You say Juliette was upset? I am not surprised."

"No, it was a shock for her, to be sure. I haven't thought what might happen next. It is too soon for them to come here. None of the bedchambers are yet ready, but my sister was so distressed I am worried now that she will refuse to come at all. It has only this moment struck me that this may not be what she wants. I thought only of myself, you see."

"That isn't true, Hugo." It was only the third time Henri had ever called him by his given name. "You were on a mission to rescue her from what you imagined to be very difficult circumstances. Of course you thought of yourself, but it was Juliette whose needs were uppermost in your mind."

"I pray to God I can make her realise that."

CHAPTER TEN

As the weeks passed Rebecca spent more time with Robert Saltaire, raising hopes in her mother's breast that memories of Hugo were fading. For Becca the days were flying by, the excursions to both Ranelagh Gardens and Vauxhall having been enjoyed immensely. She had also delighted in a succession of soirées, evenings at Almack's, visits to the theatre and numerous other entertainments. It seemed she never had a moment to herself.

Elizabeth had returned to Merivale in company with Amabel and Gil Carstairs, during which period Rebecca stayed with Lady Sawcroft. This in no way curtailed her activities, Matilda acting as a willing chaperone whenever necessary. She spent a part of each day reading to Aunt Matilda, as that lady had insisted she address her, and she became familiar with the story of *Pride and Prejudice*, a novel which had not previously come her way. Such was her amusement that she insisted Mr Saltaire read it also, so they might discuss various aspects of the plot. Both too had an appreciation of poetry, though not always admiring everything to the same degree and causing Emily Waddesdon to ask on one occasion if they'd had a disagreement.

"You seemed to be outs with each other when I observed you across the room, both frowning," she said.

Becca laughed. "No, merely we were discussing a passage from 'Childe Harold's Pilgrimage', about which we did not agree."

When Elizabeth returned from Kent she was happy to learn that her daughter was seeing as much of that gentleman as ever, but she could detect no signs of a strong attraction on either side. She recalled Rebecca's words — *it is preferable, perhaps, to look for mutual respect and contentment in one's partner* — and could not but wonder if she had decided to settle for such.

Becca did not confide in her mother her growing concern for her friend Emily. Several gentlemen had been paying court to her, but the attentions of Rufus Radcliff had been particularly pronounced. She might have thought little of it, had it not been for Henry Holland's remark that evening at the theatre some weeks ago, when he'd described Mr Radcliff as having a way with the ladies. It had not sounded complimentary, and in the light of her own experience the previous year she found herself watching more closely when they were together than she might otherwise have done. It was not for her to take such a responsibility upon herself. That lay with Emily's grandmother, but Lydia Waddesdon was perhaps herself dazzled by London society. It was only when Rebecca observed Lady Sawcroft looking quizzically at them one evening that she was able to believe that someone else at least was keeping an eye on the situation.

All thoughts of Emily fled when Harriet and Brew returned to Grosvenor Square for a while before taking Nancy into Lincolnshire to meet her grandpapa. Rebecca could not believe how much the infant had grown, and she curtailed her own activities to spend more time with her family before they might once more be on their way. The season was by now well advanced, and it wouldn't be too many weeks before she would herself return home.

"No sign of your prince yet, Becca?" Brew had asked teasingly when they had a few moments alone, flicking her cheek with his finger.

She laughed, though it cost her some effort. "The fantasy of a young girl. Sadly, very few princes have come my way. Not one, in fact. It seems I shall have to settle for someone of a lesser rank."

"Has such a one appeared on the horizon?"

"You might be surprised to learn that one or two gentlemen have been quite particular in their attentions towards me," she responded coyly.

"Not at all. You are a very beautiful woman. Have none come up to scratch?"

Becca had in fact received two unexceptional proposals: one from Henry Holland, whom she liked for his sense of humour but could not love, and another from a gentleman so advanced in years that he could have been her father, but who fancied himself a ladies' man. She had rejected both with no regret, conscious that she had caused neither pain. "I didn't think I stood a chance, you know," Mr Holland had said. "It's just that I always take such pleasure in your company." Not prince material, but charming nonetheless. They had remained firm friends. From Robert Saltaire there had been no such declaration, nor had Rebecca anticipated one. Observers might not have been able to differentiate between affection and those stronger emotions but, by deed if not by word, each had made it clear very early on that friendship was the basis of their relationship. That wasn't to say she hadn't considered such an alliance. Had Robert spoken, she might have contemplated it. She could only be grateful he had not done so.

"By the by," Brew said, changing the subject, "I received a letter from Hugo the day before we left Merivale. For some reason that has not been explained, its delivery was delayed. It had in fact been written several weeks ago. He asked to be remembered to you and our mother."

Becca turned to look out of the window, conscious of the colour flooding into her cheeks and not wishing her brother to see. "How kind of him. And is he well?"

"There was much he had to deal with, I believe. His estate and some family matters." He did not feel able to say more, for Hugo had spoken to him in confidence when discussing his findings. This recent letter had indicated that both parents had perished, but what was it about his mother that he was unable to put in writing? Brew could only speculate.

"Did he speak of returning to England?" The blood pounded in Becca's head as she asked the question and waited for the reply.

"He merely said that we had much to discuss and would do so when next we met, but he added that he had no knowledge of when that might be."

Becca was torn. She didn't know whether to be relieved or dismayed. Forcing a light tone, she said, "It is to be hoped he may come soon to visit his goddaughter. He will hardly recognise Nancy when he sees her again, she is growing at such a rate."

Brew was always ready to talk about his daughter and the awkward moment, for Rebecca at least, passed undetected.

Becca and Emily were for once sitting alone at a soirée. The younger, looking across the room to where Rufus Radcliff was in conversation with Lady Sawcroft and Lydia Waddesdon, asked bashfully, "Do you not think Mr Radcliff a very handsome man?"

Rebecca, caught in an unguarded moment, was unsure how to respond. She could easily have agreed; it was the truth, after all, and if her friend was in a mood to confide in her, it might have been a way of drawing her out. In the light of her own past experience, she thought to tread warily. "He is well enough, though I find his manner a little too forward for my taste."

Emily looked shocked. "Do you think so?"

"Well, yes. Just look at the way he fawns upon your grandmamma and Lady Sawcroft. Do you not consider it a little overdone?"

"He is merely being polite, surely," Emily said, but there was uncertainty in her voice. She had long taken her lead from Rebecca Ware and, though shocked at their difference of opinion, it made her wonder.

"He takes it beyond what is tolerable, in my opinion. It seems to me he is striving to seek favour with them, but in a manner I find overly exaggerated."

Tears appeared on Miss Waddesdon's lashes. "Oh, do not say so!"

"But why are you so upset? Do you have a tendre for him? I have observed you seem to have a particular liking for his company."

"I love him!" she replied, with all the drama that might be expected from a young lady, but Becca saw nothing to laugh at. She well remembered how, for a short while, a handsome man had been the centre of her world. She recollected too how he had nearly caused her ruin. Was she making odious comparisons and judging Radcliff too harshly?

"Then you have nothing to fear. Perhaps even now he is asking your grandmamma for permission to address you."

"No," came the bald reply.

"You cannot know that."

"I can. Rufus has declared his love for me, but he knows his suit will not be acceptable. He has no fortune, you see."

Becca was concerned but not surprised that he should have spoken out before approaching those whose responsibility it was to care for Emily. It had an all too familiar ring to it. However, she remarked, "That would not weigh with your family if his feelings were sincere."

"Grandmamma believes everyone to be after my money. No doubt Lady Sawcroft is the same."

The situation was already far more serious than Rebecca had anticipated. She hoped to be able to gain more of Emily's trust, or there was a risk of her getting into deep trouble. Drat the man! For a moment she thought of confiding her own terrifying experience and, should the need arise, she would certainly do so. Meanwhile, she must do her best to prevent Emily doing anything rash. Striving for a tone between criticism and sympathy, she said, "It was wrong of him to speak of this to you first. In your heart you know that, don't you?"

Emily's lip quivered. "He said he could not help himself."

Rebecca wondered how Radcliff had contrived to be alone with Emily for long enough to make such a declaration, for she was well-guarded. She decided to ask. "When did he say this?"

"When we last visited the theatre. You were not present, but he approached me in one of the intervals and, while Grandmamma and Lady Sawcroft were occupied with other guests, he took the opportunity to speak."

Becca thought he must have been desperate indeed to grasp such a slim chance. No doubt Emily had thought it very romantic. "Emily, believe me, I understand how you feel, but on no account must you allow Mr Radcliff to persuade you to do anything you know to be incorrect."

"Of course I wouldn't!"

Becca believed her, partly because of the indignation in her voice but more because no circumstance had yet arisen whereby Radcliff might propose any such thing. "I want you to make me a promise."

"Of course I will. What would you have me do?"

Oh dear. How to make what she said next sound neither sordid nor romantic? "You have been gently raised and, even with nearly a whole season behind you, are not entirely au fait with the ways of the world. Should anything occur that makes you uncomfortable, I beg you will come to me before you are persuaded into doing something you may later come to regret."

"You have been my guide these many weeks now. How could I not?"

There was no suspicion that Emily might prevaricate, but Rebecca had to be sure. "You promise, then?"

Her eyelids dropped but were raised again, and Emily looked unwaveringly at her friend. "I promise."

It had been some months since Rebecca had seen Hugo. She congratulated herself that she had put the past behind her. No longer was he her first thought upon waking or her last before going to sleep. That he continued to fill her dreams was something over which she had no control. She could only speculate about the problems the comte was having to deal with. She knew little of his history — only that he had been raised by an uncle in England, probably by reason of all the troubles in France years ago. She wished that he'd been able to confide in her. They had talked so easily; perhaps she might have been able to bring him some comfort. Whether or not her brother had heard from him again she had no way of knowing, for Harriet and Brew had returned to Lincolnshire.

Rebecca sighed and, as far as she was able, pushed such thoughts away. She was, for the time being, content with her lot. Two more offers of marriage had been made, both rejected, but the social whirl in which she was engaged succeeded in preventing her from constantly dwelling upon what might have been.

As yet fearful for her friend, Rebecca decided to develop her acquaintance with Mr Radcliff. He was a charming enough companion, and Becca could easily see how his manner might appeal to Emily. What she found most disturbing was that, while he conducted himself just as he ought to with others, he used every opportunity to drop a word in Emily's ear, to place a chair for her to sit on, using any and every small gesture he could to captivate her. His behaviour was exemplary, and there could be no doubt he was trying to fix his interest with her. No wonder she had fallen head over ears in love with him. But if marriage was his intention, and there could be little doubt of that, why did he not approach Lydia Waddesdon, or even journey into the country to see the girl's father? Did Becca's own sad experience make her look for problems where there were none, or was there something about his suit that was prohibitive? She wished she could speak to Gil Carstairs, who had known Radcliff at university, but he and Amabel had also left London. In the end she decided to approach Henry Holland, whom she knew had no love for the man.

"You will not mind me asking, sir, because we have become such firm friends, you and I. Some while ago, you said something that led me to believe you have no particular respect for Rufus Radcliff in his dealings with young ladies."

Henry hesitated a moment but then responded. "You will remember also that I remarked I hadn't seen him for several years. A person can change in that time."

"There is something, then?"

"It is not for me to blacken another man's reputation."

"Even when that of a young lady is at risk?"

He looked thoughtful, as though struggling with himself. "There were one or two questionable occurrences, and he was often seen in the company of some prime articles, I can tell you. Shouldn't have said 'prime articles'. Sorry. Forgot who I was talking to for a moment there."

Becca smiled. "No need to apologise. I understand you perfectly. But it isn't unheard of, surely, for students to dangle after young women when the opportunity arises. I believe it to be part of a well-trodden path."

"You're right, of course, but there was the devil to pay when he got the daughter of one of the professors into trouble. He denied it, of course, but they'd been seen together in compromising circumstances. In the end he was sent down, and he didn't return the following term. And that was the last I saw of him until this year."

"I appreciate your confidence, Mr Holland. It is easy enough to see how a young girl might be drawn in."

"You speak of a particular friend of yours?"

Even to Henry Becca didn't feel it was her place to divulge Emily's name, but instead asked, "Is there any consideration of which you are aware as to why he might not offer marriage?"

"My understanding is that he doesn't have a feather to fly with and is hanging out for a rich wife. He's tolerable enough, I suppose, but I wouldn't want him going after any sister of mine."

Rebecca had heard enough. Sadly, though, she had absolutely no idea how to proceed.

Becca had to put thoughts of Emily from her mind when her mother suddenly succumbed to a cruel illness. It began innocuously enough, with Elizabeth remarking one afternoon that she had a headache and thought she might lie down for a while. Rebecca, thinking all the gadding about was taking its toll, merely raised her eyes from her book and said, "Yes, it will do you good, I am sure," before returning to a particularly absorbing passage. It was only much later, when she knocked on the door of her mother's bedchamber, that she found her not refreshed as she had expected but tossing about, her head moving restlessly on the pillow. She raced over, grasped a hand that felt unusually hot, and placed her own free one on a clammy forehead. Seriously alarmed, she rang the bell and asked the maid to send for the doctor immediately.

"Wait a moment, I will write a note for the footman to carry to him," she said, moving to the small bureau that stood against the wall. It was not in her nature to panic, but fear had entered her body and the message she penned was filled with urgency. All the while Elizabeth did not open her eyes. Becca must have succeeded in communicating her worry, for the doctor arrived within the hour and even then apologised for being delayed.

"Now, if you will lead me to my patient, I will see if I can find what's amiss."

He was calm and composed, and for a while Becca was reassured. However, when the examination had been completed, he looked at her gravely.

"It is as well you called me so quickly. I will not disguise from you the fact that I am seriously concerned. If there are any children in the house, I would advise you to remove them elsewhere without delay."

Becca's heart was pounding. What was this thing that had struck so suddenly? "No, there are none. Just my mother, myself and the servants. What is it you fear?"

"The fever seems to have taken hold rapidly. I have come across some other cases in the past few weeks. It is as merciless as it is contagious, and Mrs Ware will become far worse before she recovers."

"Tell me the truth, Doctor. Do you in truth mean *if* she recovers?"

"You do not look like a woman who will faint upon hearing bad news, so I must tell you that this disease has claimed several lives." She gasped, but he continued, "However, I have not before been summoned to my patient so soon after the onset, and that may well count in her favour. Your mother was previously in good health?"

"Yes, certainly."

"Then we must hope it will carry her through this. I will give you some medicine that will calm her so that she ceases to thrash about so. Also some written instructions for her care, which you must follow assiduously."

"I will do whatever you say."

"Call me if you need to. I will come immediately. You have a tough time ahead of you, Miss Ware. I suggest that if you are able, you should find someone to share her nursing with you. It will do her no good if you yourself become ill."

"My mother's maid is devoted to her. Between us we will ensure she is not left alone for a moment. I will have a bed set up in this room so that, should she stir, one of us can be by her side straight away."

The doctor approved of her plan and, pausing only to tell her not to allow anyone into the house who had no need to be there, he left with a promise to call again the next day.

The situation went speedily from bad to worse. Rebecca sat by her mother's bed and watched as the restlessness increased. The thrashing about changed in manner, the movements becoming more rigid and the blood vessels showing blue in Elizabeth's neck. The hand her daughter tried to hold was snatched away as if its touch caused her pain. Becca's attempts to give her some lemonade failed miserably, the glass being struck and sent flying across the room. Only her success at administering a little of the medicine the doctor had left prevented her calling for him again in the middle of the night, but when he came the next day he reprimanded her severely.

"Did I not instruct you to share the care of your mother with her maid? Have you even left this room or taken any time to lie down on the truckle bed I see you have had brought in? No, don't bother to answer me. I can see you have not. Now," he said, softening his voice a little, "though Mrs Ware is still gravely ill, I do not expect much to change in the next twenty-four hours. While I give her some more medicine you will, if you please, fetch her maid, after which I suggest you retire to your own bedchamber and get some sleep. The maid will call you if she has reason. Once you have had some rest, you may resume your mother's care."

"I know. You're right, of course," Becca replied with wide, frightened eyes.

"Do not despair, Miss Ware. Only look after yourself, for then you will be able to look after your mother. We have a long way yet to go."

"You sound hopeful."

"I am always hopeful. It is fortunate indeed that Mrs Ware has a strong constitution, for it will stand her in good stead as she recovers. While we must remain optimistic, I wouldn't want you to underestimate the gravity of the situation. Now, do as I bid you and send in the maid so that I might explain what I need her to do. And do not return to this room until you have had several hours' sleep. I don't suppose a good meal will do you any harm either."

"I couldn't."

He looked at her with his brow furrowed, and she smiled faintly.

"Yes, Doctor, I will do as you command."

"I never command, Miss Ware. Merely I make my wishes plain," he said gently.

Becca knew that it made sense to obey him. Yes, he had made some attempt to reassure her, but there was something in his manner which gave her pause. There was no doubt in her mind that his concern for her own welfare was centred upon a desire that she might be fit enough to withstand what was to come. She would comply with his wishes, but first she needed to write to Brew. She owed it to him to let him know that their mother's life was in danger.

CHAPTER ELEVEN

Hugo slept badly the night he returned to the château, for a mixture of emotions swirled around his brain and kept him awake. Uppermost was the knowledge that his mother still lived and was well. It was for him a welcome but difficult adjustment to make, his hopes having been raised and dashed so many times. She had told her story quietly and with dignity. His sister, on the other hand, had showed fire in her eyes, resentment plain in every line of her body. Would she return to the home she had never known? There was no question that he could leave Isabelle in a peasant's house. She belonged at the Château du Berge, where she would live out the rest of her life in comfort. But Juliette had never known such a life and had been content until her world had been turned upside down. Would she be able to forgive the deception? How would it affect her relationship with their mother?

Eventually Hugo fell asleep, but it was with apprehension that he mounted his horse the next morning. However, he could not still the joy in his heart, for at last he had a family. It was apparent as soon as Juliette opened the door that his task was not to be an easy one.

"Come in," she said, turning on her heel rather than stepping aside to allow him to enter — as though she had no choice but to welcome him into her home, albeit against her wishes.

Isabelle was waiting. As she rose from her chair he took her hand, kissed her fingertips and then, because he could not help himself, crushed her in his arms.

"Maman. Maman."

"Hugo. Hugo." Her eyes, brimming with tears, looked up into his. "It is to be hoped you slept better than I, for I could not get you out of my mind the whole night."

"It was the same for me," he said, turning to his sister, who was standing apart from them, her expression impossible to read. "I have so long dreamed I might one day find you, Juliette. But for you? I cannot imagine what your feelings must be."

The relaxation of her shoulders was plain to see. It was evident she'd been preparing for battle, but his words held so much understanding that she crumpled onto the chair next to which she'd been standing. There was a bleakness about her expression. "I don't know who I am anymore. Maman and I talked long after you left yesterday and then again this morning. Everything feels so strange. Even calling you Maman," she said, turning to her mother. "I have no doubt Tante Isabelle will fall from my lips many times before I become accustomed to the change. I would be lying if I said I haven't always felt a little odd among my friends and neighbours. I have, but I accepted it as they did, enjoying the things that would never normally come the way of a country girl like me. Well, no longer like me, it seems. Having an aunt who had been in service to a grand family felt a little bizarre, perhaps, but nothing like as much as knowing I come myself from such a family. And now I no longer know where I belong."

Hugo dropped to his knees beside her and took her hands. Her speech had ended on a gulp and there was no doubt that she was, if not in a panic, much disturbed.

"Juliette, it is my dearest hope that you and our mother will come and live with me in the château. No, not immediately," he added as she tried to pull her hands away. "At present it isn't fit to house you. It has stood empty for so many years and while the work has already begun, there is much to do. There are neighbours who survived the troubles and either remained or returned to their homes. I have met a few of them in my short time here. This, if you are agreeable, is my plan." His grip relaxed and she sat back in the chair. Hugo rose to his feet and led Isabelle to an adjacent chair before laying his thoughts before them. "You will remain here while the renovations continue. No-one but we three need know of the change in your circumstances. While we wait, perhaps you, Maman, will give Juliette a greater insight into her origins. Tell her about our father. In fact, I too should like to hear about him." Nobody made reference to the fact that it might be Pierre and not Jacques who was the girl's father, but the family history would be the same. "When the time is right, and I fear it will be some weeks before I can take you home, we shall all of us be together. I will arrange one or two small gatherings to introduce you to the neighbours. Not immediately, of course, but when you have had time to become accustomed."

Juliette turned pale. It was not lost on her brother.

"You need not fear. You have nearly all the attributes required, and you are a du Berge. I have no worry about you rising to the occasion. You may not be aware of it, but you carry yourself like an aristocrat."

This was perhaps not the wisest remark. Juliette took pride in her upbringing and her background, far more so than some nebulous idea of what the future might hold.

"I don't know. I cannot say yet. I need time to think."

Hugo thought it best to change the subject. "There is an old piano in one of the rooms, covered in dust and no doubt completely out of tune. I haven't tried it myself. I do not play. Do you recall it, Maman?"

"It was my own," she exclaimed excitedly. "I haven't played for years. I wonder if I still can."

"I will have someone come to attend to it. If it is beyond repair, I shall buy you a new one and you will teach my sister."

He could see this was a temptation for both and decided he had said enough for one day but, as he left, Juliette said, "You must not assume you have won me over. I am by no means convinced that I desire this new life you are offering me."

Hugo didn't argue, nor did he put to her the obvious question. What of their mother's future, if she were to refuse?

In his absence, a letter had arrived from Brew. Hugo tore it open eagerly, keen for news and anxious to set aside his own concerns for a short time, for there was no doubt that his sister's parting remarks were a worry.

My very dear friend

It is as you surmised. Your letter, though it reached me in Merivale only the day before we left, had for some reason been much delayed in transit. Harriet and I returned with Nancy to Lincolnshire only a short time ago and are now settling into our new life here. What a difference an infant makes, eh?

I was saddened to hear about your mother. I know you had resigned yourself to her fate, but to have it confirmed must have been devastating.

It was here that Hugo had to pause. He had forgotten that when he'd last written to Brew, it was to advise him of Isabelle's certain death and it took him a moment to adjust.

I pray you have been successful in finding your sister and hope for good news next time you write. I have come to realise how important one's family is. You will recall I was estranged from my father for many years.

All that is now in the past and he dotes on his granddaughter, frequently riding over from Austerly on some pretext or other, when in truth he wants only to feel her little fist wrap itself around his finger. Nor have I witnessed anything so moving as his delight when she smiled at him. I've always regarded him as a man of few tender feelings, but I have been proved wrong.

Mama, I suspect, is missing home but remains in London with Rebecca, who I understand is having a gay time of it. Their visit will come to an end in a few weeks. My hope is that by then my sister will have formed an attachment. There are two or three who I am told are paying particular attention to her, and it would be reassuring to know she is settled in life.

Another pause as Hugo digested this information. Becca's name had fairly leapt off the page at him, and a constriction in his chest confirmed that he had not recovered from his adoration.

If there is aught I can do for you, you only have to say the word. I pray you find your Juliette.

Brew

Hugo sat for several moments with the letter in his hands, seeing not the page in front of him but an image of the beautiful woman to whom he would give his heart. It seemed she was still free, and his reasons for not declaring himself to her were no longer an obstacle. Nothing had been resolved yet, and certainly the way forward was not clear, but with his mother's and sister's affairs in hand, he felt able to pursue his own happiness. There was little that could be done in France until his home was fit for their habitation. He therefore resolved to travel to England and explain in person what had happened, and maybe by then Rebecca would have returned to

Austerly. If not, he would travel to London to try his luck alongside others who were courting her. Whether or not she cared for him, he could not know. He had taken care that their relationship remained on a friendly basis. It was time now to take a chance.

The next day he went once more to Sully-sur-Loire, and what he said brought a smile to the faces of both his mother and his sister.

"I fear I am the bearer of unfortunate news. Inept as I am, I ran my fingers over the piano keys. Anyone who has an ear for music would have groaned, I am sure. I have no doubt that even the most talented of players would not be able to elicit a tune from the instrument."

For the first time he saw a genuine smile on Juliette's face. It transformed her features entirely, while their mother said, "It is sad, to be sure, for I had such a fondness for it, but I would give much to have seen you attempt to play."

"Believe me, Maman, it was not for your tender ears. I will buy a new one for you. In the meantime, I have given some more thought to our situation. The work at the château will, as I have explained, take some weeks. Later on, when it comes closer to being habitable, I would have you come and visit. You would wish to have a say in how your own rooms are decorated and what would best suit your comfort."

He immediately observed a mulish look about Juliette's face and decided honesty would be best under the circumstances.

"Juliette, I understand you have had only a few days to become accustomed to the knowledge that you are not who you thought you were. That in itself is sufficient to think about, but we have our mother to consider. I would have a little luxury restored to her life. She has worked too hard for too many years. Her rightful place is at the château, with every comfort at her disposal. I am certain she would not come without you, is that not so, Maman?" he asked, looking across at her.

Isabelle said nothing, but the answer was written upon her face.

Hugo turned back to his sister. "You may consider my words to be blackmail in their nature, but you must see the truth of this."

Isabelle laid a hand on his arm. "Can you not see that she is frightened? You have been raised as a gentleman and I cannot forget how things were all those years ago, but Juliette, she knows nothing of the life you lead and that I once led. I will not permit you to bully her."

Hugo was filled with remorse, having been so focused on his wishes that he hadn't considered this aspect. "You must forgive me," he pleaded. "I didn't think. What a tyrant you must think me. It is all so new to all of us. Somehow we must find a solution. Maman is right, of course. You must not allow me to bully you."

Juliette's smile came again, only the second time he'd seen it, but it filled him with hope. "I can see you and I are destined to have some interesting conversations, dear brother. Yes, of us all Maman is the most important. I will consider, but you must give me time."

It was a huge step forward and gave Hugo the opportunity to impart his immediate plans. "You shall have all the time you need. In the meantime, there are circumstances which require me to travel to England for a while. You have only to send word to my steward — I will give you his direction — if there is anything you require. Also, if you permit, I will write to you while I am away and have him bring my letters to you here, if it will not cause you embarrassment. I will not insult you by asking if there is anything I can do for you. No doubt you will want to continue as before until we reach an understanding."

It was agreed, and two days later Hugo left for Winthrop and wondered how soon he would be able to go to London.

Hugo was glad to be back in England. He realised as his hired coach carried him northwards into Lincolnshire that the pressure upon him had been relentless since leaving these shores. He was now filled with the anticipation of seeing Rebecca once more, but first he would meet with Brew and bring him up to date with everything that had happened since they'd last met.

Winthrop lay not many miles from Brew's family home at Austerly and, as the carriage passed the one to reach the other, Hugo could see well how easy it was for Cornelius Ware to visit his son. He was, however, pleased to find his host alone when he finally arrived at his destination midway through the afternoon.

"Hugo, my friend, this is a pleasure indeed," Brew exclaimed, jumping to his feet as his guest was shown into the library. "Harriet is away from home at present, having ridden over to see her sister who lives nearby. You remember Gil and Amabel Carstairs? My wife takes every opportunity to ride, and while Nancy is asleep much of the time there is nothing to hold her back. I accompany her on most days, but you find me here attending to some tedious paperwork."

"I arrive at a bad time?"

"Not at all. I was looking for an excuse to cast aside the work. You must have much to tell me. Come, let us adjourn to the drawing room and I will order some refreshment for you. Accept my condolences for the loss of your mother, old man," he added, placing a sympathetic hand on his friend's shoulder.

But Brew found that Hugo was smiling as he turned to look at him.

"It seems, in spite of all evidence to the contrary, that I was in error, *mon ami*. My mother lives and is well. I have found Juliette. My whole world has been turned upside down."

"How can this be?" Brew wrung his hand and bade him sit down, pouring drinks for them both.

As Hugo laid his story before his friend, he found he was himself astonished at the course events had taken. That he had found Isabelle alive was in itself a small miracle, but the odds of him finding his sister had seemed very remote, more a dream than a hope. And then to discover the two of them together, the one entirely unaware of her heritage — well, it was an unlikely tale, and yet it was true.

"And will you persuade her, do you think?" Brew asked, Hugo having made him aware of Juliette's reluctance to enter what was to her an unknown world.

"For the sake of my mother, I must."

Hugo decided it was time to see his goddaughter and demanded to be taken to her at once. Harriet returned home soon after, and her delight at seeing the Frenchman again was evident in the way she embraced him before stepping back, with a blush on her cheeks and an apology for being so forward.

Hugo laughed. "And how many Frenchmen do you know, madame, who would not welcome the embrace of a beautiful woman?"

Harriet recovered her composure and excused herself. "I wasn't expecting visitors and must smell of the stable."

"There are worse aromas. I too will retire, if I may, for Henri will be fussing as usual. So it is with one who purports to be a servant but is as much a friend."

Brew followed his wife to her bedchamber and, dismissing her maid, imparted all that Hugo had told him. Her woman's heart was touched by such a story and tears sprung readily to her eyes. Naturally Major Ware consoled her, and it was rather later than anticipated that they joined their guest in the dining room.

"My husband has told me of the extraordinary happenings you have experienced. Who could believe such a tale? And you are preparing your home for both your mother and sister. Will they come, do you think?"

"They must," Hugo replied simply.

"I think Brew will miss you when you reside permanently in France."

"The journey is not an arduous one, Madame Ware. I would hope it is one you might undertake, as I have, for it would give me much pleasure to acquaint you with the Château du Berge. And perhaps, as Nancy grows, she may like to visit her godfather now and then."

"Well, Brew has promised to take me to France, and I can think of no better reason than to visit a good friend. Do you remain with us for long?" Harriet said and then broke into laughter. "It must seem as though I wish you gone almost as soon as you have arrived. It is not the case. Only, we understand my mother-in-law and Rebecca will soon return, and I am certain they would wish to see you before you leave these shores once more."

"Then of a certainty I will remain until then."

The next day, a letter arrived from London. Becca had written to tell her brother that their mother was desperately ill, and she implored him to join her with all speed. There was no question and Brew prepared to depart immediately.

"I will come with you, *mon ami*. You should not be alone at such a time."

"I doubt I will be good company, Hugo."

"It is of no consequence. If I can help you, I will."

CHAPTER TWELVE

When Brew and Hugo arrived at the house in Grosvenor Square, it was to discover that entry was barred to them. Major Ware, increasingly anxious for his mother's welfare, attempted to argue with his own butler, but the man was having none of it.

"Miss said that when you came I should inform her and she would speak to you from the window, no-one being permitted to enter the house, sir. I'll tell her now."

With that the door was closed on him, and the astounded owner of the establishment had to wait on the steps until his sister appeared at one of the lower windows. Hugo remained in the shadows. Eager though he was to see her, this was not the time to make his presence known.

"Are you mad, Becca? Jackson won't allow me into my own home! What is going on here? Mama?" he said, his voice breaking on the word.

"Mama is gravely ill, as I said in my letter. I don't know what I was thinking when I sent for you, for the doctor told me clearly that no-one may come inside except himself and those of us who are already here. I felt it imperative I should inform you. It was only later that I realised how futile was my summons. One of the first things he asked me after he'd completed his examination was whether there were any children in residence. His advice, had that been the case, was that they should be removed immediately, so you see how dangerous is this disease. I have to tell you that it is touch and go. There is no guarantee Mama will survive."

"If that is the case, I must insist you allow me to see her."

"You don't understand, Brew. It is highly contagious, particularly to children. Were I to permit you to see our mother and then you carry it back to Winthrop … well, it doesn't bear thinking about."

It took some persuading, but Brew was finally brought to realise the potential hazards. Rebecca begged him to remain a while in London. "Even if I can't see you, it will help to know you are close by." She tried to sound positive but was so exhausted that she could not hide the gravity of the situation, nor did she truly attempt to. "I must go. It is time for Mama's medication, and it takes the combined efforts of me and her maid to ensure she takes it."

"I will stay at White's. You can find me there if need be. And I will return tomorrow so you may tell me how she goes on."

Just for a moment Becca found some amusement in the situation. She asked her brother if he did not object to carrying on a conversation through the window, and whatever would the neighbours think? He smiled briefly in return and told her he had no patience for such pretension. She withdrew without another word and he joined Hugo, still hidden in the shadows.

"You have no need to tell me. I heard it all. Come, *mon ami*, to White's we go. A good dinner and some even better wine is what you need now."

To Hugo's distress he had not even been able to obtain a glimpse of Rebecca, for to do so would have revealed his presence. He felt no better when Brew told him how strained and tired she had appeared. Thus there was little conversation at the dinner table, both men dipping deep, each with his own thoughts. From what little he knew, it was apparent it would be a long time until he might call upon Rebecca, and he wondered whether or not to return to France. One glance at his friend's haggard features convinced him to remain a while. He had, after all, promised to help if he could.

Hugo wrote a letter later that evening, his mind clearer than it had any right to be after consuming such a quantity of wine:

My dear Miss Ware,

I write in the hope that I may relieve your mind a little of the weight you are presently carrying. You will not know that I returned to England only very recently and was staying with Brew and Harriet when your letter arrived. It had been my hope to visit London and to pay my respects to you. That is obviously now out of the question, but I have accompanied your brother in the hope I might be of some assistance to you both. He tells me that your mother is gravely ill and I wish for her recovery with all my heart. I also understand that he is unable to enter the house for fear of contracting the illness and carrying it back to his wife and child. The reason I am writing to you now is to assure you I will stay by his side, supporting him in any way I can. I hope I need not say that I would do the same for you, should the need or opportunity arise. You have only to send word.

Be brave, Rebecca (forgive the liberty of using your given name).
Hugo

He read it through twice and laid it aside. Whether or not he would send it in the morning remained to be seen.

Hugo did not accompany his friend to Grosvenor Square the next day. What would have been the point? But he did charge him with giving his letter to Becca, having decided there was nothing he could either add or that he should retract.

"I must thank you for your thoughtfulness in writing to my sister," said Brew when he returned. "Naturally I don't know the contents of your message, and neither did Becca at the time, but there was no doubt she was pleased to receive it. There is no change in my mother's condition as yet. It has only been a few days, and the doctor said it might be a long time before there is any perceptible change. Until such time as she improves, I will continue to be barred from the house. It seems ironic that I cannot enter my own home. I greatly wish I could help in the care of my mother, but Becca is right: Harriet and Nancy must be my first consideration."

Hugo knew his friend well enough to understand how conflicting were his emotions and was glad he had accompanied him to London. "It is time, perhaps, to rid yourself of an overabundance of energy," he said. "Fencing or boxing?"

There was an immediate change in the major's bearing. Here was a man who had been used to action and he approved wholeheartedly of the suggestion. "Definitely boxing. You are a Frenchman, after all. What chance would I have against you with a sword?"

"You gain pleasure only if you win?" Hugo asked, eyebrow raised in question.

"Not at all, but I like at least to have a fighting chance. You can have no idea how much I enjoy even the ability to participate now that I have overcome my lameness. There was a time I could only watch."

So long had it been since Brew had abandoned his walking stick that it had slipped Hugo's mind he'd been wounded at Waterloo.

"I had forgotten entirely. You need not think this poor attempt at gaining sympathy will result in me making allowances for your past injury."

"Absolutely not!" Brew said, slapping him on the shoulder. "Come then, let us to Jackson's and we shall see how we fare."

In the end it was Hugo who was the victor, but each felt better for the exercise.

"And now I shall take you to visit my wife's mother and her aunt. Mrs Lambert and Lady Sawcroft, both widows, reside together when in town and in the country, and both have looked very kindly upon my sister. She tells me she has informed them by letter of Mama's illness, but I would be lacking in good manners if I did not pay them my respects."

"Two elderly ladies! You terrify me."

Brew laughed in return but assured Hugo that the women concerned were neither old nor terrifying. And so it was that two very much less than intimidating ladies were delighted to receive a call from the major and the comte.

"It is kind of you to come. Is there any further news of Elizabeth?" Lady Sawcroft asked when they were all seated in her comfortable withdrawing room.

"I believe nothing more than Rebecca has already informed you. I am concerned not only for my mother but for my sister also. This has come hard upon her and she appears exhausted even after only a few days. Heaven knows what a toll it will take on her, for Mama is in the care only of her and her maid."

"You have seen your sister?" Louisa asked. "My understanding was that no-one was permitted into the house. Naturally Lady Sawcroft and I both offered our services, but we were told it was impossible."

"And impossible it is. Conversation was only achievable because Becca leaned out of a window to speak to me, but even I was barred, not only from seeing my mother but from my own home."

"Where are you staying?" Louisa asked.

"The comte and I are at White's, and it is there you may find us should the need arise."

"Tell me, then, of my daughter and granddaughter. How were they when you left Winthrop?"

It needed nothing more to bring the smile back to Brew's face, and as they talked Hugo took the opportunity to conduct a little light flirtation with Lady Sawcroft, whom he found to be absolutely charming.

"What a naughty boy you are," she said, rapping him on the knuckles with her fan but hugely entertained. Hugo's thoughts drifted for a moment back to where his own mother and sister were living in a peasant's cottage in Sully-sur-Loire. Would he ever be able to return them to such society as this?

It was with trembling fingers that Rebecca opened Hugo's letter. She sat beside her mother's bed, staring at it in wonderment before unfolding the page. It wasn't long and there was little to raise her hopes on a personal level, but he was here. In England. And he wanted to help her. She held the paper against her cheek, marvelling that not many hours since, it had been in Hugo's hands. How typical of him to be at Brew's side, and to assert that he would remain as long as needed. She read it again and again, pinning her hopes on his promise: *I hope I need not say that I would do the same for you, should the need or opportunity arise. You have only to send word.* Silent tears poured down her cheeks as her pent-up emotions gave way to release. The letter was not from a lover but a friend, and that was what he had been to her all those many weeks ago. As before, she could not know his feelings for her. What she did know was that he would be there in her time of need, and when her mother recovered, she would see him again. She turned and took Elizabeth's for once still hand in her own.

"He is come, Mama. He is come."

The arrival of the doctor interrupted this pleasant reverie and she couldn't help but notice that the poor man looked exhausted.

"You will forgive me coming so late, Miss Ware. I have been summoned in all directions this day. How is our patient faring?"

He didn't wait for an answer, though she gave one, moving directly to the bedside to examine her mother. He looked grave and struck fear into her heart as he shook his head slowly from side to side.

"She is worse?" she whispered, her anxiety plain to hear.

The doctor glanced over his shoulder, almost as if he'd forgotten her presence. "No, though she is no better either." He sighed and straightened up. "But it is early days, and I see no cause for undue pessimism at this stage. To be frank, I had expected her to be worse, such has been the pattern I have seen in others. It is far too soon to raise your hopes, but neither is it time to despair. My advice is that you continue as before. What of you, Miss Ware? You appear to have managed to find time to rest."

She smiled. No need to explain that any softening in her features was due to the letter she had so recently received. Instead she showed the doctor to the door, promising to do his bidding, and handed her watch over to the maid. She didn't immediately seek her bed but sat instead at the escritoire in her chamber and sharpened her quill before settling down to write. Her first letter was to Brew.

Dearest Brother

I must first give you news of our mother, though really there is none to speak of. The doctor has just left. He tells me there is little change in

Mama's condition but I took some reassurance from his assertion that it would by now have been far worse had it been following the pattern he has seen in others. In spite of all my previous protestations, I must say that I would call for you immediately if I believed your presence and the sound of your voice would reach our mother sufficiently to make a difference. The doctor is still insistent you stay away. It hasn't been a week and yet it seems like half a lifetime to me.

Do you think we ought perhaps to send for my father? I fear for his own health were he to undertake the journey from Austerly, but is it right that we keep him in ignorance? You told me you hadn't informed him of the severity of Mama's illness before you left Lincolnshire, but would he ever forgive us if the worst were to happen? It does not bear thinking of. I will be guided by you in this matter.

You cannot know what a comfort it is to me to see your face when I come to the window, and how much strength I am able to draw from the fact that you are but a short distance away and can come when I need you. How kind of the Comte du Berge to have accompanied you. I have no doubt he will help keep you from dwelling too much on something you cannot at present influence. Should you go about town at all, please convey my respects to any of my friends and my apologies for any commitments I am at present unable to honour.

That is all, I think, until you come again tomorrow.

Rebecca

She turned next to thoughts of what she might write to Hugo, biting her lip in consternation, for it was important she strike the right tone. Then she laughed at herself. And what right tone would that be? She was merely replying to his kind communication. But still her pen remained poised for some while before she began.

Dear friend

What a lovely surprise to find you are now in England. I trust you have succeeded in sorting out your affairs and that we will see more of you. Not, of course, that I am able to see you at present, but I would have you know that your letter brought me great comfort in what is a truly difficult time. My poor mother is fighting a deadly illness and there is little I can do to aid her, but to know there are those who would support me in my time of need gives me courage. Your care for my brother moves me more than I can say. I can only guess how much it must irk him to remain inactive at such a time and I rely on you to distract him in so far as you are able, even though I have no right to ask such a thing of you.

Her next several moments were spent contemplating whether or not she ought to say what had suddenly sprung into her thoughts. Would he consider it bold of her to ask such a thing? No matter, she had thought it and now it had to be written.

It occurs to me that you may accompany Brew when he comes to Grosvenor Square. Should that be the case, I would ask that you do not stand aside but join him at the window. My world has shrunk considerably, and it would give me so much pleasure to see another friendly face.

I think we know each other well enough now to put convention aside. I am sure neither of us need regard the accepted niceties of Society under the present circumstances and so, Hugo, I give you rein to be free with my name as I have been with yours.

Rebecca

Like Hugo before her, Becca twice read through what she had written before folding the page. She then rang the bell and asked that both letters be delivered to White's, where she knew they would ultimately find their intended recipients. She then lay fully clothed upon the bed and fell into an exhausted and dreamless sleep.

Hugo and Brew received an impromptu invitation to a soirée that evening, a fellow member of White's explaining that he had not known the major was in town and, though it was bound to be a tedious evening, his mother would be delighted to receive them.

They laughed but promised to attend, having nothing else planned. Few of those present were known to the pair, but they were delighted to see Louisa and Matilda, and brought them up to date with the news, or lack of it, about Elizabeth. A rather flamboyant-looking woman of a similar age, perhaps slightly older, approached and was introduced as Lydia Waddesdon, some sort of connection of Lady Sawcroft's. She in turn introduced them to her granddaughter. The poor girl was looking a little fraught and, when the rest were all engaged in conversation, Brew contrived to draw her slightly apart.

"Forgive me, Miss Waddesdon, but I wondered if something was ailing you?"

"Oh no, Major Ware, though it is kind of you to ask. It's just that … well, I wonder if you would mind conveying a message to your sister. She has been very kind to me, and I understand she is not going about at the moment."

"That's correct. Our mother is unwell, and Rebecca has undertaken her care. What would you have me tell her?"

"Nothing. Only that, she said, if ever I should…" Emily was falling over her words, and it was evident she was incapable of putting together a whole sentence.

"Would you wish me to convey your respects?"

"Yes, that's it. Of course. If you would tell her … if you might say that there is something pressing I need to ask her about, and perhaps I might write to her."

Brew smiled kindly upon her. The poor child, for she seemed no more than a child, was like a frightened kitten. And then her grandmother looked up, and Emily fluttered to her side without another word. What little experience Brew had of ladies of her age told him that each small thing assumed enormous proportions, and probably there was little to worry about. However, he couldn't help feeling a little disturbed and vowed to repeat the conversation to Becca the next day. Meanwhile, the evening was yet young and he went off in search of the card room, where he found Hugo already engaged in a game. Instead of indulging in play himself he stood at his shoulder, just as happy to be an observer. On the way back to White's, Hugo asked if he was acquainted with Robert Saltaire or Henry Holland.

"I recall hearing both names, but I cannot put a face to either. Were they present this evening?"

"I believe you were in conversation elsewhere when I was introduced. Each professed a particular interest in your sister."

"Ah, yes. One is the gentleman in whom my mother had great hopes for Becca. Of the other I know nothing."

Hugo's heart plummeted. He had hoped Rebecca had not attached herself to another. Was it possible he was wrong? Her letter to him had been couched in affectionate terms, but it was impossible to read any stronger emotion in her words. Had he returned too late? He slept badly that night. Nonetheless, there was an excitement about him the next day that he was barely able to control. Today, after all this time, he would at last set eyes again on the woman he loved.

CHAPTER THIRTEEN

She's as beautiful as ever, was the first thought that went through Hugo's mind when Rebecca appeared at the window. There were little worry lines about her eyes which he wished he could smooth away, but nothing could detract from her perfect features and thick, dark blonde hair. She looked at him and smiled before turning to her brother to impart what news there was about their mother. Surely there had been something in her eyes that was for him alone? Or was he merely a besotted man, intoxicated by her beauty?

It seemed there was little change in Elizabeth's condition. "This is cause for some small celebration according to the doctor," he heard her say. "He was almost optimistic, which of course gave me cause to be optimistic too. No, Brew, you are still not permitted entry, for he considers her still to be contagious, but she has ceased her thrashing about. Perhaps, in a day or two…"

"Then I must wait in patience, no small achievement for a man of my temperament. Hugo here will see to it that I am adequately occupied."

Becca turned to him at last, and the smile she bestowed upon him lit up his world. Surely he could not be mistaken.

"Hugo, it has been a long time. You cannot know how glad I am to see you." Simple words. He could not imagine how she prayed they might convey much more.

"So much has happened since last we met, and I had to leave Merivale in haste. My hope is that your mother will soon be recovered sufficiently for me to call. I have so much to tell you.

Things I wish to explain." It was as much as he could say with Brew standing by.

Mindful of his conversation with Miss Waddesdon the previous evening, Brew passed on her message as requested.

"She appeared worried, you say?" asked Becca.

"Trapped would be a more apt word, in my opinion. She seemed to be relying upon you for the solution to some problem that is bothering her."

"Oh no! Brew, I beg you to call on her."

"I hardly know her!" he protested.

It was Hugo who said, "We will find some pretext. I will come with you. If your sister wishes you to go, you must comply. It is evident there is some cause for concern, *n'est ce pas?*"

Rebecca looked at him with gratitude for his quick understanding. "It is indeed so, though I cannot impart to you something that was said to me in confidence. Only tell Emily to remember her promise to me. Will you do that?"

"Of course. Is there anything else?"

To the surprise of both men, Rebecca turned away from the window before returning moments later and apologising. "Forgive me, I have been pacing the room, for I don't know what to do. I would go to her myself, but I am forbidden to leave the house. No, Hugo, there is nothing else. I must pray it is enough."

They went immediately to call on the Waddesdons, stopping only at St James's Square to avail themselves of the direction and explaining that they had a message to convey from Rebecca. Matilda was no fool and could detect straight away that there was a certain urgency about the request. This was no social visit, she was certain.

"Is anything amiss?" she asked, straight to the point and impossible to evade.

It was Hugo who replied, "I know of nothing precisely, but Miss Ware was concerned and it seemed the situation carried some urgency."

"I will come with you." It wasn't a request. "In that way, you may be assured of some private conversation with Emily, for I shall draw her grandmother aside."

There was no arguing, and indeed it would have been foolish to do so. She would be able to contrive so that a potentially awkward situation might be carried off with some ease. They waited while her carriage was sent for and in the meantime were hugely entertained by this redoubtable woman. Mrs Waddesdon was extremely flattered to receive a visit from them, and between them Hugo and Brew succeeded in putting her granddaughter at her ease. Soon enough, an opportunity arose for them to fulfil their commission, but as they spoke all colour left her cheeks.

"What have I said to distress you, mademoiselle? Can I fetch you some water?"

"No, sir, I thank you. It's just that, well, you caught me off guard for a moment. Please tell Miss Ware that I have not forgotten my promise. Whether or not I am able to honour it I am not yet sure, but I beg you will not convey that part to her, for she has enough to contend with at the moment. It is doubtful in any case that she could aid me in my current predicament." She caught herself up on a sob. Both men half rose from their chairs, but she indicated that they should remain where they were. "No, please don't. Grandmamma must not know there is anything amiss." She seemed by sheer force of will to collect herself. She then thanked them for their trouble and withdrew, not in body but in spirit. There was no reaching her after that and, having indicated to Lady Sawcroft that they had fulfilled their charge, they left soon after.

"Well?"

They were seated in the carriage once more, and Matilda wasted no time in demanding to know what had been the outcome.

"I fear we were only successful in distressing Miss Waddesdon even more. It is not a message I am eager to carry back to Miss Ware."

"You must not do so on any account, Monsieur le Comte. Just tell her you have passed on her communication. Brew," she said, turning to her nephew-in-law and speaking in a quiet tone that conveyed the severity of what she was saying, "I am truly afraid Miss Waddesdon is about to make just such an error as your sister did last year. I will keep a watchful eye on her, but there is a strong possibility that I may require your services in the near future."

Brew cast a sharp glance at Hugo. His friend had no knowledge of what had happened, and he was quite cross with Matilda for committing such an error of judgement as to speak so in front of him. There was little he could say without making matters worse, so he merely replied, "I am as always ready to oblige you in any way I can."

She had seen the glance and was immediately aware of her mistake. She turned the subject and hoped that her slip would not produce unsought consequences.

Hugo hadn't missed Brew's sudden look, nor the slight undercurrent between the other two. What could possibly have occurred that had involved Rebecca? Evidently it was something serious. Naturally he could not ask the question outright. If his friend chose to confide in him, well, that was another thing. Nor would he be able to inquire of Rebecca herself, even had they been able to have private conversation. He could only pray she wasn't carrying a burden and wished more than ever that he might be able to take her worries upon his own shoulders. There was little he could do meanwhile other than continue to offer his support.

The two men returned to Grosvenor Square, keen to inform Becca that they had delivered her message. She seemed to be reassured by the knowledge that Emily was holding true to her promise. She accepted it readily enough, for in fact something had occurred to distract her from her friend's welfare.

"I am so very glad you are back. I was about to send a message to your club. There has been a change since you were here only a few hours ago."

"Mama?" His anxiety was plain to hear.

"Yes, Brew. After you left I went to sit with her again, only to find she was thrashing about in a way that convinced me she was in terrible pain. It seemed she couldn't find a comfortable position and, had I not been there, I am certain she would have thrown herself off the bed."

"*Mon Dieu!*" exclaimed Hugo.

"Exactly," she said, looking at him. "You may imagine my fear. I sent immediately for the doctor, and he came within the hour." She paused and bestowed a beautiful smile upon them both. "Would you believe that by the time he arrived, the episode had passed, she was calm once more, and even my inexperienced eye could see she was better?"

"Thank God!"

"Yes, Brew, thank God indeed. She has not spoken yet — she is barely conscious, but she has at last opened her eyes. Only for a moment, and she didn't recognise me, but the doctor has assured me she is now over the worst and he has every confidence in her complete recovery. She is sleeping now. What do you think of that, then?" Becca finished triumphantly.

"I think you could not have given us better news. You will know that your letter put me all on end, not knowing whether or not to send for Papa. I have been in a quandary ever since, for there was certainly the prospect that we might have two sick parents on our hands. I refrained from sending for him and can only be glad I did so. When Mama is fully recovered, we will carry her home by easy stages, though I fear it will bring your trip to London to an end a little sooner than you had anticipated."

"As if I cared for that!"

"And did the good doctor say that Brew might visit your mother?" asked Hugo.

Rebecca threw him a saucy look. "Did I not say so? Actually, the answer is no." Brew looked crestfallen. "But he did say that in a day or two you might be permitted entrance to her bedchamber. If her progress is as hoped, you may then come to her bedside. In the meantime, tomorrow I will be happy to welcome you into your own drawing room, and I can tell you it will relieve me greatly not to have to speak to you through a window. The doctor believes Mama to be no longer contagious. His concern is that we do not tax her strength too quickly."

Hugo grasped his opportunity by asking, "And may I be permitted to accompany your brother?"

"*Naturellement,*" she replied in his own language. "You have been as much a part of this episode as we. We owe you a debt we cannot repay."

"*Ce n'est rien.*"

"On the contrary. You have been instrumental in preventing my brother from breaking down his own front door. That in itself must be considered an achievement. I look forward to seeing you both tomorrow. For now, I must return to my mother."

And with that she was gone. As they returned to White's, Hugo could only think that she did not bear the appearance of a woman who was carrying a burden. He wondered again what had occurred a year past and whether or not he would ever find out.

Rebecca sat by her mother's bed all night, wanting hers to be the first face Elizabeth saw when she properly regained her senses. In spite of her exhaustion, for she had only snatched a little sleep here and there, she made a special effort with her attire. She told herself she would have committed to equal endeavour for any prospective visitor, but she knew that in truth it was because Hugo would be coming with her brother to Grosvenor Square.

Though she had been listening for their arrival, Brew had mounted the stairs so quickly that his entry into the room caught her by surprise. He grasped her in a hug that said more than words ever could and then set her away from him as the comte entered. Hugo bowed deeply over Rebecca's hand and kissed her fingertips. His lips lingered for longer than was conventional, but he was unable to help himself. Regardless of his friend's presence, he said with ill-concealed passion, "Miss Ware, I am delighted to see you again at last."

She laughed, something she hadn't done for a long time, and said, "Tell me, sir, in what way I have offended you that I am once again reduced to Miss Ware."

Any stiffness vanished in that moment, and they were once again at ease with each other as they had been all that time ago at Merivale.

"Now, be seated, both of you, for I must tell you that since last we spoke Mama has twice opened her eyes. The first time she squeezed my hand, and the second she smiled at me. The doctor warned me that her recovery will take some time, one aspect of the illness being that it will have drained her of energy. He said also, having already visited her this morning, that you may go today and sit with her for a few minutes if you wish."

Brew needed no further bidding and fairly raced from the room. Left alone together, neither Rebecca nor Hugo suffered any feelings of embarrassment. Such a look he cast at her, and she at him in return. He made no declaration of his love for her. Now was not the time. There was no doubt on either part, though, of the strength of the connection between them.

"Has my brother been driving you to distraction with his impatience?" she asked with a sympathetic smile.

"Let me say only that it has been challenging at times to channel his thoughts away from despair. Like any man of action, it does not sit with him well to be inactive."

"You have my everlasting gratitude for being able to do so."

He said quite simply and with no side, "It is not your gratitude I desire."

It was understood. She turned the subject, asking that he tell her of some of his travels since last they'd met, and then saying, "No, it is better you wait, for Brew might return at any moment and you did say you had much to tell me."

"Certainly more than I would be able to do in this short time we have together. I assume that he will wish to move back into his own home. I will remain for the time being at White's, but I hope you will permit me to call on you. Perhaps to take you for a drive, for a walk will quickly tire you out after all you have been through."

"What a poor creature you must think me, though I suspect you may be right," Becca replied, honesty compelling her to acknowledge the truth of his observation. Before any more was said they looked questioningly at each other, both having heard loud and insistent knocking at the front door. "I wonder who could be calling with such urgency?"

She was soon to find out. Lady Sawcroft was shown into the room and unceremoniously sat down and bade them do the same, they having risen at her entrance.

"We must put niceties aside. Rebecca, I have only an hour since received a visit from Lydia Waddesdon in just such a state as you now see me. It seems that Emily has fled with that Radcliff fellow. I'm not surprised, of course. Lydia didn't keep such a watch on her as she ought, and now you see what has become of it."

Becca paled and looked at Hugo. "She told you she remembered her promise to me," she said, a question in her voice.

He had the grace to look guilty. "She spoke of the possibility of not being able to honour that promise."

"And you didn't tell me!"

Lady Sawcroft interceded. "It is of no use you flying off at the comte. It was I who directed him not to tell you. I hadn't suspected things had come to such a point, and I didn't want you being further distressed with all you had to contend with."

It was at this moment that Brew returned, and the joy at seeing his mother was soon replaced by consternation when all was revealed to him.

"I must go after her. Surely he will not have carried her off to Gretna Green. He must know there are those who would waylay them long before they could reach that destination."

"You're right, of course," said Matilda. "It's marriage he's after, I make no doubt, but the border is far too risky a proposition."

"Then where?" Rebecca asked.

Hugo, with no previous knowledge of the situation, was quick to grasp the implications. It was he who said, "He has a home in the country. It is there he will have taken her. His intention will be to keep her there until her reputation is in ruins and her family have no choice but to agree to their union."

"Are you sure?"

"Nothing is certain, Miss Ware," he replied, addressing her thus on account of Lady Sawcroft's presence. "It seems to me to be the most logical, if it is her fortune he is after."

"He will not carry her to France?" Awful memories came flooding back but Brew, forgetting his friend, assured her the circumstances were not the same as those she'd experienced with Dorian Fletcher a year previously.

So that was it, thought Hugo. He looked at Becca and saw the fear in her eyes, and his heart went out to her. He could not reassure her, not in front of the rest when he hadn't yet sought her hand. He only hoped that his expression would tell her he could be relied upon. But then Brew was speaking once more and contact between them was broken.

"I must follow them."

"No, *mon ami*, it is I who will pursue them if you will but give me the direction. After all your mother has been through, you must remain here."

"I can't ask such a thing of you."

"You didn't. Now, don't be a fool, Brew. Make haste, for I must overtake them before nightfall. Do you know where he lives?"

"I will find out for you."

"I'll need a horse."

"That too."

Between them, the two men made the necessary arrangements and in as short a time as was possible, Hugo was on his way. Rebecca, by no means comforted by Hugo's look, for she knew how dreadful was the thing she had done, could only see the hope for her future happiness leaving with him.

CHAPTER FOURTEEN

Hugo headed west out of London. Supposing he was wrong? What if Radcliff had indeed journeyed north to Scotland or was yet carrying Miss Waddesdon eastwards, towards the coast? It didn't bear thinking about. Even if his pursuit was in the right direction, he was still hours behind his prey. The distance to his destination was such that it could be covered without changing horses, as long as he paced himself. It was for him the better option, as his mount was strong, steady and seemingly fearless.

He passed the time not in consideration of what he might do when he overtook his quarry but in contemplation of the woman he had left behind. He had not been impervious to the look of despair in Rebecca's eyes when her secret had been revealed. In any other circumstances, he would have done his utmost to reassure her. He had no idea whether or not the man in question had succeeded in his aims or at what stage Rebecca had been rescued. What he didn't doubt was that she had been a vulnerable young woman and that her vulnerability had been taken advantage of. It didn't for a moment alter Hugo's feelings for her. Their earlier exchange of glances had said as much as any words of love might do, but had his last look been enough to convince her of his devotion?

It was mid-afternoon by the time he reached his destination, a country house of imposing lines, not large but speaking of its owner's standing. And then, as he came nearer, he could see both house and grounds were neglected. Was this the reason Radcliff needed to marry an heiress? Hugo secured his horse and pounded on the front door. There was no response, hardly surprising under the circumstances, as he was pretty sure the owner would have instructed his servants not to admit any visitors. Or maybe he'd been wrong, and Emily hadn't been brought here at all. He shuddered at the thought.

After trying again with the same result, he began to walk around the house and was much relieved when he came to a room where the curtains were not drawn across. He could clearly see a table, dressed ready for a meal. Hugo was not in the habit of breaking into someone else's house, but since there seemed to be no other way he searched for an open window into the dining room or a faulty latch. Luck was with him, and he clambered over the threshold. He passed through the door into the hall and immediately heard the sound of a woman whimpering. The noise came from behind the door of a room opposite, and he lost no time in striding over and turning the handle. It gave way under his pressure and he entered the room to find Emily struggling in the arms of one who was to him a stranger but whose identity was beyond doubt. The couple sprang apart.

"What the devil!" the man exclaimed.

Hugo ignored him. "Ah, Miss Waddesdon, I trust you are ready for me to restore you to your family. They are, as you may imagine, concerned for your welfare, so the sooner we leave the better."

"Thank God. Oh, thank God!" She collapsed in tears on his shoulder, but he set her aside, for Radcliff was coming towards him, arms raised. An anger such as he'd never known ran through Hugo's veins. Was this, or something like it, what Rebecca had experienced? Rufus Radcliff had no chance to plant his blow, for an iron fist laid him out on the floor. Two men appeared in the doorway, a footman and one who bore the appearance of a butler.

"Ah, you will see your master has suffered a mishap," said Hugo. "Be so good as to arrange for his carriage to be brought to the front door with fresh horses, and I will remove the young lady so that you may attend to him."

He spoke with authority and, with Radcliff unresponsive, they ran to obey his orders.

Hugo turned back to Emily. "Miss Waddesdon, I trust you have suffered no hurt."

"No, I am safe, thanks to you, sir. I couldn't … I didn't…"

"You have no need to explain. Did you bring with you any belongings you wish to retrieve?"

"There was no time. He told me, he said…" Her voice faded away again and both turned as Radcliff stirred and began to recover his senses. He struggled to his feet, hot rage marring his otherwise handsome features.

"How dare you…"

"I wouldn't if I were you," Hugo said quietly as the other moved towards him. "I have ordered your carriage to be brought round so that I may convey Miss Waddesdon back to London before nightfall. I will leave my own mount here to be retrieved. I think the sooner this sorry mess is forgotten, the better. If you mention one word to blight the lady's reputation, you will have me to deal with — and believe me, I will find you, wherever you may choose to hide." He inclined his head slightly and turned his back to his host. "I believe that is the coach. I fear it will be a difficult journey for you, Miss Waddesdon. I must drive you myself, and I am assuming without seeing that it is an enclosed carriage, but you will perhaps be better alone with some time for reflection," he finished kindly.

Hugo offered her his arm and she took it without another word. They went into the hall, not even turning to take their leave. He bestowed some largesse upon the butler and requested that his horse be taken care of until it could be retrieved. Then, settling Emily on the seat and covering her knees with a blanket that was to hand, he said gently, "Don't worry. I'll have you home with as much haste as I am able."

It had been Hugo's original intention to take Emily back to Grosvenor Square, where Rebecca might take care of her, but he'd had second thoughts. For one, Mrs Ware was still not recovered. For another, it was possible his darling would be even more distressed in the light of her own experience. Remembering what Matilda had said about Lydia Waddesdon, he made the decision to take Emily instead to St James's Square.

Arriving many hours later, he handed the weeping young woman into Lady Sawcroft's arms, her caustic comment being, "Just as well you've brought her here. Her grandmother, having failed her entirely, has declared herself absolved from all responsibility, washed her hands of the situation and left London."

"Oh no!" Emily wailed.

"Now, don't you fret, young lady. I will take care of you."

It was late, but Hugo still had one obligation to fulfil. The house in Grosvenor Square appeared to be in darkness and he wondered if all had retired, but his knock was answered and he found Brew in the library, waiting for news. When the comte walked in alone, he sank back onto his chair and ran a hand through his as ever unruly hair.

"You did not find them, then," he said in a desperate tone.

Hugo responded with a broad grin. "Indeed I did, and Miss Waddesdon is even now with Lady Sawcroft."

Brew stood again and wrung his hand with enthusiasm. "I knew I could rely upon you."

"Having just accused me of failing?" the other said with a laugh. "I will leave you now, but I shall call again in the morning, by which time I hope you will have apprised your sister of the happy outcome. *À demain.*"

Rebecca passed an indifferent night. She'd heard the knocker the previous evening from the sanctuary of her bedchamber. It was faint at so great a distance, but she'd been listening for it. She'd previously considered waiting up, but the possibility of Hugo bringing news so quickly had seemed remote. It didn't stop her hoping, though, and when he arrived — it could surely only be him at such a late hour — she'd been tempted to leap out of bed and race downstairs to where she knew Brew was still waiting. What prevented her was her inability to interpret the look Hugo had earlier sent her on hearing of her shame, for such she still thought it. Had the information destroyed those tender feelings that had been so apparent only a short while before? She could not know and therefore remained where she was, for she could not face his contempt. Had they needed her, they would surely have called. She pulled on a robe, crept over to the door, opened it a little way and waited until she heard Hugo leave before hastening to confront her brother.

"Did he find her? Is she safe?"

"She is, my dear. Hugo took her straight to Matilda. And would you believe that Lydia Waddesdon has abandoned her and gone home? So Emily is to remain at Sawcroft House, and none will be the wiser. My mother-in-law's discretion can be relied upon absolutely."

"Of course. I remember how kind Louisa was to me under similar circumstances. So Emily will have two good and capable women watching over her."

"Yes, and her grandmother's absence can be easily explained by some crisis which caused her to leave Emily in Matilda's care. No one will remark at that."

"I must go and see her. She will be distraught. And what of Radcliff?"

"Laid out on the floor, apparently, and all the fight gone out of him. Hugo thinks he will say nothing. It will do his own reputation no good, after all. Go back to bed now, and I will speak to the doctor when he comes tomorrow. With his permission, I will remain here with Mama so you may go to St James's Square."

They went upstairs together, entering their mother's room to find the maid asleep on a truckle bed against the wall, it no longer being necessary to watch Elizabeth every moment. Moonlight shone in through the window, throwing a bright light onto where she was sleeping. They were reassured and went no further for fear of disturbing the maid. Before they parted company, Brew promised his sister that if the doctor did not come, he would remain with their mother, for even to their untrained eyes it was evident the case was no longer desperate.

It might have been thought, after all the worry of the previous days and the added stress of Emily's flight, that Rebecca would have fallen into a deep slumber, but such relief eluded her and in the end she was relieved to see the dawn breaking. Ringing for her maid and wasting no time, she left the house as soon as the morning was sufficiently advanced for her to pay a call at St James's Square, thus avoiding a meeting with Hugo. Emily hardly dared look her in the face, so ashamed did she appear to be at the breaking of her promise, but Becca went straight to her, enfolding her in her arms and telling her not to worry, that she was safe now. Both shed tears, and Louisa and Matilda left the room, knowing it would be easier for the younger women to exchange confidences without their presence.

"You must be so disappointed, after all I said to you, after I promised to come to you when I had the need."

"We both know I was forbidden to allow anyone to visit," Becca soothed.

"I could have sent a note."

"Something I am sure you would not have done, not wishing to burden me when my mother's position was so precarious."

Emily acknowledged the truth of it but appeared to be inconsolable. Rebecca judged it time to confide in her, to present proof positive how well she understood the situation.

"You are blaming yourself, I know, but responsibility lies not with you but with your abductor."

In a tremulous voice, so soft that Becca could hardly hear, Emily said, "I agreed to go with him."

"But my understanding is that, by the time the comte overtook you, you were regretting that decision."

"It was horrible, Becca. You cannot imagine. He promised to cherish me and then he grabbed me in the most awful way and would not release me when I begged him."

A loud sob was proof she'd had a terrible fright, and Rebecca cast her mind back to her own similar experience.

"Believe me, I know how you feel." She paused, moving from her chair to sit beside Emily on the sofa and taking one hand in her own. Taking a deep breath, she said, "I know because only a year since, I was myself in the same situation, except I discovered later that the man in question had no intention of marrying me."

"What!"

"While I believe Rufus Radcliff truly wanted to wed you, no honourable man behaves in the way he did. I had my suspicions a while ago, for I was able to observe the two of you and I could see how he was drawing you in. I should have told you of my circumstances then, but I hoped to protect you without the need to do so. It is I who owe you an apology, not the other way around. Like you, I was rescued when all seemed lost. You will not recover immediately. It was months before I could look in my glass and tell myself truly that the fault was not mine, and believe it. So too will you. I am sorry that your grandmother has failed you, but you could not be in better hands than you are today." She laughed gently. "Lady Sawcroft and Mrs Lambert will bully you mercilessly; you will be dragged to the theatre or to a dance when all you want to do is hide in your room. And you must do as they say, for moping will not help you. Sadly I will not remain long in London, for when my mother is sufficiently well, my brother and I must carry her home to Austerly. Until then, I will see you when I can and I will leave knowing that you will come through this. You may not believe me now, but you will discover an inner strength you are unaware you possess and, after time, a peace and contentment that will carry you forward. Now, dry your eyes and let us call our hostesses, for I mean to go home. However, I will return later so that we may walk together in the park."

"I couldn't," Emily pleaded.

"But you must. For my sake. I have been cooped up in the house for days on end, and I rely on you to bear me company. All my dependence is upon you."

Rebecca had then only to leave and to pray that by the time she got home, Hugo would have come and gone. Her interview with Emily had been draining, and she didn't feel able to face him until she'd had time to collect herself. It would not be long delayed, she knew that. What the outcome might be, she could only guess and hope.

Brew was sitting by their mother's bedside as promised when she arrived. He had only left his post, he told her, to exchange a few words with Hugo, who had come in her absence.

"He said he'd hoped to have an opportunity to speak to you, but there was obviously something on his mind and he didn't stay."

Her brother's words struck fear into Becca's heart. She could imagine only too well what was bothering Hugo and was grateful that he was man enough to want to tell her himself rather than just withdraw. She dreaded facing him.

"He said he'd be back this evening. Meanwhile, Mama has been awake twice, and for a few minutes at a time. She spoke your name and looked about the room, evidently searching for you. I assured her you'd only stepped out for a while and she settled back into a peaceful sleep, as you can see."

Rebecca dragged her mind back from thoughts of Hugo and sat on the other side of the bed, taking Elizabeth's hand. It was sufficient to cause her to stir, and the smile that lit her features was reward enough for all the hours of worry her daughter had endured.

"What a fright you gave us," she said gently. "But that is all passed now, and the doctor said we might carry you home when you have gained enough strength to travel. What a change we will see in little Nancy when we return."

Brew nodded. "Harriet writes that I will hardly recognise her, and I have seen her more recently than either of you. I must admit I miss them both."

"Soon," Elizabeth said, her voice barely above a whisper, and it was evident even that was an effort.

"Not, however, until you are entirely well, Mama. Brew, why do you not go ahead of us? We can follow as soon as may be."

He wouldn't hear of it, of course, maintaining that while his family were safe and well in Lincolnshire, a few days here or there would make little difference and there was no way he was going to permit his mother and sister to travel with a stranger in attendance. There was no moving him, and Becca was relieved. She was somewhat overcome by exhaustion and would be happy to leave all the arrangements in his hands.

True to her word, she collected Emily from Sawcroft House and together they walked to the park, their maids following closely behind. With summer so close upon them, the day was hot but thankfully a light breeze was blowing. Everywhere early flowers were bursting forth, leaves unfolding on the trees, lightening the mood of both women.

"Now, hold your head high, Emily. No-one is aware of what has happened, and if anyone should enquire after your grandmamma you must say she has been called home. Ah, and here is Mr Holland bearing down upon us. Good day, sir. It is a fine afternoon, is it not?"

"All the more so for seeing you, Miss Ware. Good day, Miss Waddesdon. I must hope, since you are amongst us once more, that your mother is well?" he asked, turning back to Rebecca.

"Not well, but improved to the extent that I may now leave her for a while and venture out of doors. You cannot conceive what a treat it is for me."

They talked amiably for a while before he moved on and, during the course of their walk, several others of their acquaintance stopped to converse with them. The excursion had done them both good, Emily going so far as to say that she couldn't have believed she might feel so much better.

"Aunt Matilda speaks of holding an impromptu soirée tomorrow evening and before we came out this afternoon, I couldn't have imagined being able to face such a thing. It seems less daunting now. I do hope you will come."

"So it is Aunt Matilda now? I swear that woman is the softest in nature, try though she might to convince everyone she is a tyrant."

Emily giggled. "You mustn't tell anyone, but I am so much happier staying with her than I was with Grandmamma. It is ungrateful of me, I know, but it seemed to me she spent more time pursuing her own pleasure than looking after me."

Rebecca, satisfied that Emily had more resilience than she might have hoped for, acknowledged what she'd said and promised she would attend the forthcoming soirée.

CHAPTER FIFTEEN

For the sake of Rebecca's sanity it was as well her mother was awake and, if not sitting up and paying attention, at least aware of her surroundings and eager to be entertained. Sunlight streamed through the window, but Elizabeth was protected from its rays by a screen which had been carefully placed for just that reason. The illness had taken a great toll and it was important, the doctor had said, to keep her mind occupied while her body recovered. To this end, Becca retrieved the book Elizabeth had been reading before she'd been struck down.

"Would you like me to continue from where you left off, for I see you have marked the page with a ribbon?"

Her mother was too weak to say much but indicated with a shake of her head and a movement of her hand that she would prefer to begin again. She drifted in and out of sleep and, each time she did so, Becca would pause and allow her thoughts to dwell on the Frenchman who had stolen her heart and whom she feared would this evening cut the connection between them. There had always been a certain frankness between the two of them, and she knew he would not present a dishonest front. She hoped it would be a quick departure and that she might grieve alone. Her thoughts were so firmly focused on Hugo that on one occasion the book she had laid on her knees fell to the floor with a bang and woke Elizabeth from her slumber. Becca continued to read, but when her mother dozed off once more she put the volume safely on the counterpane. Somewhere, buried deep, she still felt guilt at being so easily misled by Dorian Fletcher. Would Hugo remain to witness her distress, not out of malice but in a misguided attempt to console her? If he were to linger she could always excuse herself, she supposed, saying her mother needed her.

The interview, for such was how Becca imagined it, proceeded like nothing she had anticipated. Brew having taken her place at their mother's side, she was alone when Hugo was shown into the drawing room. Before she had time to prepare herself, he strode across the carpet and gathered her in his arms, crushing the cream muslin gown she had chosen especially.

"*Ma chérie*, I had not dared hope I might find you alone."

Little kisses were planted all over her face, on her cheeks, on her eyelids and, finally, on her mouth. Becca allowed her pent-up anxiety to find relief in a flood of tears. She stroked his hair. His chin. One trembling finger touched his lips.

"I thought, after what you learned about me yesterday, that the love you felt would have died." But she took his hands as the fluttering settled and she felt an unfamiliar contentment deep within her.

Hugo laughed, pleased at last to have been able to give vent to his emotions. "Did you? Then you thought wrongly. All the while as I rode to Emily's rescue, I could think of nothing but you. I didn't know the circumstances of what you endured and still I do not, nor do I wish to unless you feel the need to tell me. I was filled with a rage such as I have never before experienced. The thought of you, frightened and alone. You may imagine my anger. What I am certain of, what I thank God for, is that someone came to your aid in just such a way as I did Miss Waddesdon's yesterday."

What Rebecca said next wasn't a test but an observation. "But you don't know if that aid came in time."

"Nor do I care, except insofar as it might have caused you unhappiness."

Becca was quick to reassure him. "My rescuer did come in time. I should say rescuers. Harriet Lambert, as she then was, for she and my brother were not yet married, and Gil Carstairs. They overtook us on the Dover road and carried me back to the sanctuary of Merivale. You may imagine now why I have such a fondness for the place. It was there I recovered my composure sufficiently to face the world again."

"Of Carstairs' resourcefulness I have no doubt. You must know I met him several times in Paris before he and Brew returned to England early last year. As for Harriet, a formidable woman if ever I met one. You were in good hands."

"Indeed I was. But Brew mentioned that something was bothering you. Naturally I thought…"

Hugo became grave all at once. "You thought wrong. There is on my mind a thing that must be dealt with, and because of it I must leave you again." He took her hands once more. "Last time I was a coward. This time I will not leave without your promise that you will become my wife. It is possible I will be away for many weeks, for I must return again to France."

"I will wait, Hugo. For as long as it takes, I will wait. My life without you is existence only, and but a short time ago I thought I had lost you forever. Of course I will marry you."

Heedless in each other's embrace, neither heard the door open or Brew enter the room. They sprang apart when he said, "Well, I'm glad you two have got that sorted at last. For a Frenchman, my friend, you have been remarkably slow in coming to the point."

"Well, now that I have, I would ask that you shake my hand. Wait, though. Must I ask your permission to wed your sister?"

"Not mine. Nor even my father's. Rebecca is of age and may do as she wishes, and it seems very obvious to me what her wishes are on this occasion. So, you told me this morning that you wished to speak to us both. What has occurred?"

Brew moved to sit on a chair and Rebecca and Hugo sat side by side on a sofa, making as much of their short time together as they could.

"I have this morning received a letter from my mother."

Rebecca looked up quickly, realising she had no knowledge at all of Hugo's family. "One must assume from your demeanour that it is not good news."

"Certainly not what I hoped for." It was time for Hugo to give his fiancée some knowledge of his background and what had come to pass when he was last in France. For the moment, he gave her only a brief outline so that she might understand the urgent need for him to return. "So you see, *ma belle*, that I discovered not only a sister but also my mother, whom I believed to have perished."

"But that's wonderful!"

"It is, but it carries with it its own problems. Juliette is not of a mind to come to the Château du Berge. When I left them in Sully-sur-Loire, it was in the hope that she would come to terms with the circumstances, if only for our mother's sake. It seems there is a young man."

"Would you not wish your sister to be as happy as we are?" Rebecca asked, obviously puzzled.

"Of course. But the man in question is a farmer, not an aristocrat. I'm certain you perceive the difficulties. The match would be unequal by birth, but not so by upbringing. If Juliette comes to her rightful home, it would be true to her birth but not a life she is accustomed to lead. There would be much for her to learn. And the farmer? What of him? You see the dilemma."

"Oh, poor woman."

"Yes, Rebecca, but I must think also of Maman. Juliette is urging her to return home while she remains living the frugal life she has been raised to. They must not be parted!" Hugo tore at his hair, frustration obvious in every contour of his body. "And so I must return in haste to try what I can to resolve this muddle."

Brew stood up and walked over to his friend, placing a sympathetic hand upon his shoulder. "It is a task I do not envy you. When do you go?"

Hugo turned from brother to sister, seeing despair in both their eyes. "Tomorrow. I must go tomorrow."

Brew had no hesitation in leaving the two alone together. It would be weeks before they might see each other again, and it would have been cruel to deprive them of this last opportunity. They spent their time not in close embrace but talking to each other.

"In truth, I know everything and nothing about you, Hugo. That you were raised in England by your uncle, yes, but not how that came about. Before today I had no notion of your mother and sister. It seems you believed your mother to have perished?"

"Yes, and I had no knowledge until recently that I had a sister."

He went on to explain what he'd found hidden in Pierre's desk, though he kept from her Isabelle's liaison with his uncle. That was not his secret to tell, and in any case no purpose would be served by his doing so.

"You may imagine my astonishment upon learning of Juliette's existence. I had accepted the loss of my parents. How could I not, in the light of what my mother's letter had suggested? It served only to confirm what my uncle had always said to be the case. But that Juliette might still live? That I might find her? These were questions that tormented me. Even then, I knew I was in love with you, *ma chère*. You must have known when we were at Merivale. But I could not declare myself to you. Who knew what I might find? Or how long it would take? So I left you, hoping that in some way you recognised my feelings, and that they were returned."

Salty droplets fell silently down Rebecca's cheeks. She was moved, both by Hugo's story and the knowledge that her instincts had served her well, even in her despair. She'd known. Of course she'd known — only, she hadn't allowed herself to hope. And now he was here, holding her hand, wiping away her tears. Her heart beat fast in her bosom.

Hugo was talking once more, this time about his family home. "The château was, is, in such a state of disrepair that it will take many months to restore it sufficiently to take you there." For a moment, he hesitated before saying, "You will come and live with me in France? You could bear to leave your family?"

"My home is where you are, Hugo. In any case," she laughed, "it seems to me no great ordeal these days to travel to and from the Continent." She became serious once more. "What will you do if you cannot persuade Juliette to join us?"

"I cannot say. There seems to be no satisfactory solution either way. It is why I must return as soon as I may. Oh, my darling, how I wish I could take you with me."

Rebecca spent some moments trying to demonstrate to him that it was her wish also before deciding to tell Hugo the whole of her own sorry story, praying he would understand.

"I was twenty when I first came to London, but I could as well have been a girl of fifteen or sixteen, so little did I know of that world and the people who inhabit it. You will know from Brew that my family led a life almost of seclusion after the death of my sister. As well as our grief was the seemingly impenetrable wall between my father and my brother, and then Brew left us to join the army. The only person left of anywhere near my own age was Gil Carstairs. I took him as the model for all. You know Gil. Kind, gentle and with a sense of humour. I imagined all others to be the same."

She paused, for the next part of her tale would be more difficult.

"It is hardly surprising, then, that when a man professed to have feelings for me I did not question whether or not he was genuine. He promised marriage. Persuaded me to run away with him, not across the border into Scotland but to France. I found out to my everlasting shame that marriage formed no part of his plans. Had Harriet and Gil not overtaken us, I would have been lost. I can never repay them."

Hugo's arm was resting along the back of the settee behind Becca's shoulders. She had lowered her head, the full impact of what had happened coming once more to the fore, but he used the fingers of his free hand to raise her chin and turn it towards him.

"You were an innocent. You have nothing to feel guilty about. Is that why you were so aware of Miss Waddesdon's situation?"

She marvelled at his understanding. "It was indeed. I watched him seduce her, saw her fall in love with him. The outcome was almost inevitable. She was good enough to confide in me, hence the promise I spoke of. Sadly, with Mama so ill, I was not there when she most needed me. If it hadn't been for you…"

"I am happy to have been of help, and you may trust me not to say anything about what occurred."

Becca gave him a blinding smile. "I know that, Hugo. You are a gentleman."

They spent but a few more minutes demonstrating their appreciation, each for the other, before he rose, pulling her up with him.

"It is time."

"Go then, before I beg you to stay."

Hugo left without another word. Becca was sad but she did not cry, for there was an inward happiness which she knew would carry her through until they should meet again.

With Hugo gone and her mother no longer needing constant attention, Rebecca took up the reins of her social life once more. There was a certain glow about her that heightened her already beautiful features. It mattered not to her that she couldn't share the reason for the added rosiness in her cheeks, the new spring in her step. No announcement of their engagement had been sent to the *Post*, as there had been no time. She was glad of it. It wouldn't have suited her to be receiving the congratulations of her acquaintances without her fiancé at her side.

A mischievous impulse sent her on a shopping spree, taking Emily as her companion. After all, she told herself, who knew where she might acquire her wardrobe once she was married and in a strange country? She had no qualms about encouraging her friend to join her. It might perhaps distract her from her recent worries. A new bonnet, for instance, was just the thing to light up a young girl's face.

Either Lady Sawcroft or Louisa Lambert, or sometimes both, would accompany the younger women on these excursions, Matilda declaring that she liked nothing better than spending someone else's money. Emily was delighted and Becca was gratified to find that, far from retiring into her shell, she was displaying an appreciation of some of Lady Sawcroft's most outrageous remarks and a new aura of confidence that she had lacked before. "I must tell you, Aunt Matilda, that I will most certainly not purchase the blue muslin unless you buy that shawl," the young lady said audaciously during one of these trips. "It suits you admirably, and it would be a crime to leave it behind."

It wasn't long before Becca discovered the source of her friend's seeming change of personality. On more than one occasion when visiting Sawcroft House, she found Robert Saltaire there before her. At any party he would be found at some point at Emily's side. What a change from the rogue who had pursued her before. Robert was quiet, attentive, and Rebecca could be certain he would never behave in a way that might frighten her. So the confirmed bachelor was courting, was he? He was perhaps a little old for the object of his desire, but it may be that she would be better off with a more mature man to guide her and upon whom she could lean. Becca had an opportunity one evening, when Emily was engaged in conversation with another, to say with a decided twinkle in her eye, "Tread gently, my friend. She is a flower easily crushed."

He didn't pretend to misunderstand. Hadn't their relationship always been open and honest? "As if on eggshells, Miss Ware. She will come to no harm at my hands, I promise you."

She knew it to be true, trusted him implicitly and, with her own newfound happiness and imminent return to Lincolnshire, she was more than happy to know that she would be leaving Emily in the care of one who would guard her from every breeze and shelter her from every storm. In short, she could hand over the reins of responsibility to another. A week later, she and Brew accompanied their mother back to Austerly, each grateful to leave the ever increasing heat in the capital.

"Your brother has done well, Rebecca. I swear he couldn't have found more comfortable accommodation on our journey home."

Mother and daughter were walking in the garden of the inn where Brew had engaged rooms for them. Elizabeth was still very weak but a few steps were beneficial and Becca, after not too many minutes, persuaded her to sit in the shade of an apple tree.

"Ha! He is a soldier, Mama. Everything is conducted as a campaign. And here he is with the promised lemonade."

All three Wares were comfortable, sitting for some time in silence, each with their own thoughts. Brew, though he didn't speak, couldn't disguise the excitement he felt at the prospect of seeing his wife and child again. Rebecca was lost in reverie, wondering how Hugo's quest was developing and hoping to receive a letter from him soon, for he was aware of their plans to return to Austerly. Elizabeth took the opportunity to doze in the afternoon sunshine that filtered through the branches and leaves of the tree. Later they ate a hearty meal, the journey having left them all with a heightened appetite. When Elizabeth retired early, brother and sister played cards until it was time for bed.

The next day followed a similar pattern, and the afternoon of the third found them turning into the drive of Austerly, each of them relieved to have reached their destination. Brew remained only long enough to pay his respects to his father before continuing on to Winthrop to be reunited with his family. Upon his departure, Rebecca said, "Be assured I shall ride over tomorrow to see Harriet and Nancy."

"Not at all. I will bring them here, for I know Mama is longing to see them." He paused, one hand on the rein, the other taking hers. "I am happier for you than I can say, Becca. Whatever the outcome of Hugo's endeavours, I know you will be happy with him. Until tomorrow, then."

He was gone and she retired to her room, standing at the window and looking out onto the summer afternoon. She had witnessed the reunion of her parents with unlooked-for happiness. These two had been given a second chance in life. Never would they forget their lost child but at last, after all these years, they were pulling together. Other thoughts flittered through her mind as she changed her dress before joining them for supper, but she had never been more content. She could not imagine what pattern her life would take, but she would be with Hugo. It was enough.

CHAPTER SIXTEEN

As Hugo waited in a Dover hostelry for the tide to turn, he couldn't help feeling akin to the Roman god Janus, part of him looking back, the rest looking forward. But this time his thoughts of Rebecca were full of joy. How different from the last time he'd stood here, thinking perhaps he had lost her forever, feeling the uncertainty of his situation that had prevented him from claiming her as his own. As he stepped on board an hour later, he was still reflecting on how much things had changed. There was so much new joy in his life, but the road he had yet to travel would be strewn with obstacles, for there seemed no easy solution. Though Henri kept assuring his master all would be well, he could offer no resolution to the dilemma that faced him. He hoped the way ahead would be less choppy than the waters over which he now passed.

"Do you think it will take long for the château to be made sufficiently habitable to bring your wife home?"

Hugo had naturally confided news of his betrothal to Henri. Indeed, he could not have stopped himself from doing so, such was the change in his demeanour. The valet was happy for him. These last few years had been somewhat turbulent for his master, and he would be glad to see him settled in the same way as his friend, Major Ware. Both had experienced pain and loss. It was to be hoped that was now at an end.

"I can't remember when I have undergone a more uncomfortable passage, Henri," said Hugo when they stepped off the boat. "Tomorrow we will continue our journey but tonight, after my stomach is settled, we will enjoy a hearty meal."

The rest of the way proved to be uneventful, and by the time they reached Château du Berge Hugo was heartily tired of the road. Urgent though his mission was, he chose to remain there the next day, rather than proceed immediately to Sully-sur-Loire. Instead, he spent the time inspecting all the alterations that had taken place in his absence, and he was delighted at the progress. The gardens, which before had been a tangled mess, had been cleared and summer was in full bloom, insects murmuring as they flew from flower to flower. Reparations had been made to the wall, which contained a profusion of roses he had not even known were there. The small lake which had previously been covered in slime now appeared inviting, and he wondered if any fish had survived. If not, he would add stock, for he enjoyed a bit of angling. Beyond that his land sloped away down to the river, an area he had not so far inspected but which he was looking forward to exploring. Should the way prove accessible, he might even take his rod down there. Dramatic as the changes were outside, inside was almost unrecognisable from what he had perceived that first time he had stepped into his family home. The steward had wrought a veritable miracle, and he knew sufficient had been achieved that he might bring his mother and sister home, if only both were agreeable. Tomorrow he would find out.

With the morning sun beckoning him, Hugo could not help but feel optimistic as he rode towards the village. The day was joyful. Surely his quest would end well? He maintained his feeling of well-being only to have it dashed as his mother drew him into the cottage, her face saying more than any words. She embraced him with enthusiasm, but as she sat beside him her expression was grave. He looked around but there was no sign of his sister.

"She is gone?" he said, fear rising to the surface.

"*Non, mon fils*. Juliette is proud and honourable. Whatever her decision, she would confront it, and you, full on. It is not in her nature to run away."

"Then…?"

"She is on the farm. It is how she met Auguste in the first place. He was looking for aid in picking the fruit last summer. It is his habit to employ itinerant workers in the season, but Juliette is not of course in that category. Being a local girl, she remained when the rest had left. I had no perception until recently that her affections were engaged. And his."

"You are certain of this?"

"I see it in her eyes, Hugo."

"So, this Auguste, are you saying he is a landowner and not the common farmer I was led to believe?"

"You have become very high," his mother answered disapprovingly. "Pierre was always very conscious of status. I see he has instilled the same in you."

He was a little surprised to hear her speak so of her lover, but there could be no doubt her years of living such an altered existence would have changed her perspective on life.

"Not so, Maman. I am merely trying to be practical. As a common farmer, the match would be unequal in the extreme. If this Auguste is a landowner, it is an entirely different scenario."

Hugo could see that Isabelle was looking distressed. "That is twice now you have called him *this Auguste*. As if he is beneath contempt."

Hugo sought to reassure her. He spoke gently, trying to explain that his concern was for her and Juliette both. That the opportunity was there for them all to come together as a family. "Surely, Maman, you could not bear to be parted from her, even more because she is now aware of your true relationship."

"Parted? How so? The distance between here and the château is not so great."

He was taken aback. "Are you then happy with this prospective alliance?"

"Hugo, stop for a moment and think. My world has undergone many changes. I was fortunate enough to have the love of two men, both of whom I adored. I had my children and then you, my son, were taken away from me, together with Pierre. I was bereft. And after, to save her, I had also to give my baby away. Such a scrap of a child, her life hardly begun, and she too was lost to me. Your father died in terrible circumstances and I was lucky to survive, but there could not have been a greater disparity between my previous existence and the one I came to lead. At least I was granted the opportunity to watch my daughter grow, to give her guidance where I could. The years passed in a strange contentment. The life here is simple, but that doesn't mean it isn't good."

"You approve then of this marriage?"

"How you do twist my words, Hugo." Isabelle smiled, but it was a poor attempt. "Before you came and found us both, I would have been more than content. Auguste is not of the aristocracy, but he is a man of some substance. Juliette would want for nothing and she would be happy. And then everything changed, and I began to dream of going home. At first I was carried away, not considering what it might mean to *ma fille*. If you think about what you and I have had to contend with and the opportunity that has now presented itself, try to imagine how alien all this must be to your sister. We both know what we are missing, but Juliette does not miss what she's never had. And because it is outside of her experience and she is happy with what she does have, why would she even wish to change?"

It gave him pause. For the first time he began to see his coming not as a blessing but as a bane. No wonder his sister had reacted in the way she did. More so when she was already devoted to her farmer. The feeling of optimism he had carried with him to Sully-sur-Loire had abated somewhat but had not deserted him entirely. It would appear that his vision for the future was blurred at the edges, but there were other possible futures. If he trod carefully there was no need for him to be estranged from Juliette, but he must first meet Auguste. Of one thing, though, he was sure. He had gleaned from his mother that her wish for herself would be to return home. He would make that wish come true.

Hugo spent some two or more hours with his mother, he describing in detail several of the changes that had already taken place at the château and she — sometimes with a faraway look in her eyes, sometimes looking directly into his with such eagerness — asking him about this and that. It seemed the walled garden had been a particular favourite. "I considered it my own, for your father preferred the larger expanses of the estate. I can still recall the scent of the roses."

"Then you must come soon, for they are in bloom at the moment." This brought a momentary halt to their conversation, for neither knew if Juliette would accompany her or no. "She will come to visit, surely, even if not to remain?"

"I cannot speak for her, Hugo. She makes her own decisions."

"Then we must not seek to put pressure upon her. I realise, so intent was I upon my own wishes, that I have handled the situation badly. I will leave you now and hope that my sister will be here when I come again. Should you have the opportunity — without distressing her further, you understand — I would ask that you reassure her of my good intentions and respect for her own wishes. In the next day or so, I hope we may consider a time for you to come home, for I would value your suggestions before I make further reparations." He could see that Isabelle was looking alarmed and realised the cause immediately. "Not for you to remain, of course. That cannot happen until things are resolved with Juliette one way or another. I would hire a carriage to bring you and you may return the same day if that is your wish. I hope that my sister will come also." He smiled as he perceived the humour in such a situation. "If only out of curiosity. She is a woman after all, *n'est ce pas?*" And he went away laughing, happy to see the smile return to his mother's face.

When Hugo returned to Sully-sur-Loire two days later, he received a much warmer greeting from his sister than before. It seemed his mother had done her work well, and he was delighted and relieved to observe this other side of Juliette, one he had not before witnessed. There was a definite smile lurking in her eyes as she said, "Well, *mon frère*, it seems Maman is anxious to visit the château. It is to be hoped you have done all to her satisfaction, for I make no doubt she would have you tear it all out and begin again."

Hugo responded in kind. "I fear you are right, which is why I am hoping she will come and give me instruction before things progress too far. If I have chosen the wrong shade of purple, it might prove to be a disaster."

"Purple!" Isabelle exclaimed, alarm writ all over her face. This caused brother and sister to laugh, for the first time at one with each other.

"He is teasing you, Maman. At least, I hope he is."

"You are right, of course, but it is true that I would value her opinion. And yours, Juliette. If you could bring yourself to accompany our mother, I would be pleased and honoured."

"Pah! Honoured indeed! I shall come, of course. What woman could resist?" She grew more serious. "I would ask in return that you come with me to meet Auguste. You are aware how things are between us and, while I will go where my heart leads me, I'm sure you understand, I would like my brother's approval, if you are able to give it."

"Had you not requested such a meeting, I would myself have asked for it. I have been hasty, I know. So much has happened in so little time. I did not stop to consider. You will forgive me?"

Thus were the seeds of their relationship sown, each ready, willing even, to accommodate the other. It occurred to Hugo that he hadn't told Isabelle or Juliette about Rebecca. Now was not the time — there was too much else to the fore — but he realised all at once that he wanted to share his happiness with them. His sister must be feeling the same. He tried to imagine how he would have felt had his family objected to his choice of bride. No wonder Juliette had reacted the way she had.

"Shall we say tomorrow, then? I will send a carriage to collect you and be ready for your return later in the day. If you are seeing Auguste in the meantime, perhaps you will arrange a time to suit you both when I can visit him. I am at your disposal."

And so it was arranged. As Hugo rode home, he contemplated all that had occurred so far. He thought he had redeemed himself. He hoped so. He wondered what Rebecca would make of it all, and he smiled.

My dearest darling

I send this letter to Austerly, for surely sufficient time has now passed for you to be home. There is much to tell you and little also. I have seen both my mother and my sister and have spent time in an attempt to recover some ground. So selfish was I that I considered only my wishes without thought of what plans Juliette might have for her own future. It took my mother's words to apprise me of my error. What an egotist I have been, setting so much store by my position in society.

I have yet to meet Juliette's Auguste, a farm owner and not, as I had first thought, a farmhand — you see, I do it again! I had no idea I was so arrogant. It is arranged that I will visit him soon and I suspect from what little I have heard of him that pride in his heritage will more than match my own. We come from different spheres, but does that make the one any better than the other? You will observe I am in a reflective mood and anxious that he should accept me, for I am sure there will be no parting the two of them. And who am I to say they should be parted?

Tomorrow they come to the château, Maman and Juliette. I cannot imagine what my mother's thoughts must be. Trepidation? Elation? Both, I imagine. Forgive me, ma chère, but so suddenly were we parted, you and I, that I had a little time to consider our own future. As yet I have not mentioned our betrothal. Such an important announcement must await the right moment. You are ever in my thoughts, but as to the practicalities, well, it has only just occurred to me that I am asking you to share your future home with a woman of whom you know very little and who until now you have not even met. I hardly know her myself, though it is certain there is an emotional connection between us. I pray this is not too much to ask of you, for I can see no other solution and I am not prepared to give you up. Sooner a cottage with you than a château in the Loire Valley.

Hugo did not think it politic to mention that he had no notion either as to what his mother might make of such an arrangement. After all these years, would she be prepared to return to the home where she had once been mistress, only for that position to be taken by another?

Do I have your permission to speak of our engagement? Will I return to England and carry you off as my bride? There is much to be done here and nothing to be accomplished before tomorrow, or even until after I have met Auguste. Later, whether things be sorted or not, I fear I cannot bear to be parted from you for much longer and must fly to your side.

Jusqu'à plus tard

Hugo

The next morning was fine and sunny, and Hugo hoped it bode well for the coming day. He drove the carriage himself, humming as he went. There was no way he would permit a stranger to escort Isabelle and Juliette to the château. In any case, his mother's reaction when she saw her old home might take a number of different forms and he wanted to be close at hand to support her, should the need arise. Both ladies were in fine fettle when he arrived in the village, and one or two people emerged from their cottages at the appearance of such a magnificent carriage in their small community. Hugo's previous visits had always been as a rider and had caused no such interest. He hoped it wouldn't be a cause of embarrassment. He had come in an open conveyance, choosing to give them as sweeping a view of the approach as possible, and there was no doubt there would be much speculation amongst the inhabitants as to why two of their own were being transported.

There was little conversation on the way, for even though Hugo was able to look over his shoulder when his horses were at a walk, the attention of his passengers was taken up in surveying the unaccustomed scenery through which they passed. As the château came into view, he did glance back in time to see his mother clasp her daughter's hand. Probably quite tightly, though of course he could not tell. She didn't look apprehensive. More her features displayed expectation, causing him to feel a little more at ease. Drawing his horses to a halt, he jumped down and held up his hand to support Isabelle as she descended.

"It is like going back in time, *mon fils*. It was on such a day that your father brought me here for the first time."

Her eyes were glistening with memories of which he had no part, but they were happy tears. He turned to Juliette, handing her down to stand beside their mother.

"It is beautiful," she breathed. "Since first you came to see us, Maman has tried to describe this scene to me. I have a lively imagination, but in no way did I anticipate such magnificence. It is no wonder she has such a fondness for the place. I cannot wait to see more."

With one woman on each arm, Hugo guided them up the steps and through the entrance but then Isabelle, breaking free, ran like a child from place to place. She returned after some minutes with eyes seemingly grown to twice their natural size.

"You spoke as if the place was in ruins, Hugo, but you have done so much already to restore it to its former glory."

"But you haven't even seen all the rooms on this level, Maman. How can you know?"

"It matters not. Come, Juliette, let me show you this room behind the stairs. It was a favourite of mine because it gives onto the garden, and the views are incomparable."

The staircase in question was a rather imposing structure, with stone steps and ornate wooden bannisters, not yet restored. The steps rose to the next level, where they split into two separate flights. Their shoes tapped noisily on the flagstone floor and Juliette threw a decidedly saucy look at her brother as she was dragged away by Isabelle. Asking a footman to remain in the hall, should they return that way, Hugo made his way by a different route to the garden, where he was reasonably certain his mother and sister would appear. He had judged correctly, for it wasn't many minutes until they appeared on the terrace, as yet also in need of repair. Isabelle was heading for her beloved rose garden.

"Take care, Maman. There are many cracks in the stones," warned Hugo, but he laughed, for there was no holding her. He could not have wished for a better response. Nothing was more certain than that she felt she had come home. But what of Juliette? Was she overwhelmed? Would she visit after her marriage to Auguste, something Hugo was now persuaded would happen even before he had met him? She hung back as their mother raced ahead, heedless of the hazards beneath her feet.

"I've never seen her so happy, Hugo. It would be cruel of me indeed to even consider trying to convince her to make her home with me, for be assured that was my intention," said Juliette.

Hugo chose his next words carefully, for they were of great importance to their future relationship. "It is understandable. You had never seen her in her natural environment. You couldn't have known this is where she is meant to be. I made a similar error when I considered bringing you here willy-nilly." He took her hand in both of his. "Even though I haven't met Auguste, I know you belong with him. I will tell you something now that I haven't yet mentioned even to Maman. Before I left England, I became betrothed. Her name is Rebecca, and when I am not with her I feel a part of me is missing. If that is what you feel, and you have made it clear it is so, then you must follow your heart's desire."

For the first time since they had met, Juliette pulled her hand away and embraced her brother. No more words were necessary, though many were later said, but for the time being each was content. All would be well. They had come together, this family. They would not be torn apart again.

Having had her fill of the garden, for the time being at least, Isabelle proceeded to the rest of the property, followed by her children. It being vast, this took a long time. Some of Hugo's alterations were approved, and his mother's expression was enough in other cases to tell him it was not so.

"At least there is no purple for me to contend with," Isabelle said, acknowledging his previous jest.

"If there is anything that truly offends you, Maman, I will be happy to make changes."

"Not yet, for I would have to live here again for a while to feel the atmosphere. It is so important when furnishing a room, don't you think? I had forgotten, having lived in such a small space for so long, how daunting it can be."

"Are you distressed?"

"No, Hugo, just a little overwhelmed. Give me time."

"And you, *ma soeur*, are you also overwhelmed?" Hugo's anxiety was plain.

Juliette, it seemed, had recovered from her initial brusqueness and teased him instead. "It is large, of a certainty, but I have become accustomed to the size of the rooms in the farmhouse and, though the building itself is not as grand, it is nonetheless extensive. No, don't look so shocked, Hugo. I haven't seen *all* the rooms."

He rather liked this coquettish side of his sister and would have chosen to continue in this vein, but they had reached that part of the château in which the secret chamber was housed. Hugo was fortunate enough to catch Isabelle's arm, for she had stumbled and might well have fallen.

"Forgive me, Maman, rambling on in this way. I ought to have realised what distress it might cause you to come here, for was it not from this very place that you left home so long ago?"

"It was, my son, but having come this far I must proceed to the end."

She moved in front of him determinedly, and though she gasped when they came to the entrance, she did not fail. Her children followed her in and Juliette paled when she saw the space in which her mother had been hiding.

"It is grim indeed."

"There were many like it, my child, I can assure you. Those were frightening times in which to live."

"Anne-Marie's cottage must have seemed like a palace to you after this."

Isabelle smiled and put trembling fingers to her daughter's cheek. "Not a palace, but certainly a haven. What astonishes me, seeing it now," she continued, turning to Hugo, "is that it lay undiscovered all these years. Many of our valuables travelled with you and Pierre to England, for to have sent you there in poverty would have been hardly better than you remaining in France. But my jewels, they were still here, you said."

"*Oui*, and when you are ready I shall take you to the library and show them to you."

"There is no time like the present, *n'est ce pas?* I think I will not come here again," she added, as the hidden door was closed behind her.

Hugo watched in amusement as the two women pored over the array of trinkets and baubles that had been spread across his desk. There were some beautiful pieces, of that there was no doubt, but some were to his mind rather more gaudy than his inclination permitted.

Isabelle smiled. "Your father did not always have the best taste but chose to shower me with gifts. It was not for me to deny him his pleasure."

Juliette, on the other hand, stared in amazement. Never before had she seen such things.

"You do not approve, my dear? I hope you will admire this, for I wore it at my wedding and it is my wish that you will do the same." She had pulled a single row of pearls from the rest. Simple, beautiful, elegant. There was no mistaking her daughter's reaction or the faraway look in her eye as she imagined the wedding day to come. Isabelle turned then to Hugo. "The rest must be for you to do with what you will. They are part of your inheritance."

"*Grands Dieux*, Maman, not while you live, which I hope will be for many years to come. You are worried about my finances? I can assure you that my uncle was a shrewd investor and that which you sent with us to England was multiplied many times over. Now, enough of this nonsense. I think it time I drove you back to Sully-sur-Loire, for the day has passed quickly. I would wish to be able to return here while it is yet light, there being little moon to speak of tonight."

"Of course. I hadn't realised." Isabelle's eyes were glowing still as she tenderly replaced each piece in its box.

Hugo placed a hand on her arm. "There is something else I haven't yet told you. Both of you." He turned to Juliette as she reluctantly put the pearls back in the box until the allocated time. "I was nothing less than a brute to you when first I learned of your attachment to Auguste. It should not have been so, and I hope you will one day find it in yourself to forgive me. I ought to have understood, you see." A beaming smile lit up his features. "I am myself betrothed to the most wonderful woman in the world, and I cannot wait for you to meet her."

"By all that's marvellous, you have kept this to yourself well, my boy," exclaimed Isabelle.

"I know, Maman, but the time wasn't right. It was imperative that we resolved our problems here first without this added information for you to deal with."

"Deal with! What a fool you are. I could not be more pleased. This wonderful woman, she has a name?"

"Rebecca. She is the sister of my closest friend."

It was Juliette who broke the spell, as a new thought occurred to her. "But you cannot expect Maman to live here at the château with a woman she doesn't even know! At least not straight away."

"Of course I can. It is her home."

"She has lived with me these past twenty or more years. Perhaps she should continue to do so for a while."

"What difference here or at the farm? Her position will be the same." Hugo's voice had risen with his frustration.

Juliette, her temperament a match for his, said, "It is not the same. She knows me and she knows Auguste. She has never in her life met this Rebecca."

Hugo burst into laughter and it took him some while to control himself, his sister growing more red in the face with every passing moment, but Isabelle smiled.

"Your brother is laughing because I reprimanded him severely for calling Auguste *this Auguste*, and you have done precisely the same. This and that. Do not quarrel, my children. We will find a solution to our problems. One thing is for certain. Though it may not have been so in the past, our future lies together. Now come, Hugo, or it really will be dark by the time you return."

CHAPTER SEVENTEEN

The days passed pleasantly enough for Rebecca. Elizabeth's recovery was taking longer than anticipated, and part of each afternoon was spent in a pastime they both enjoyed. A persistent weakness made the holding of a book for any length of time a task rather than a pleasure for her, so her daughter continued to read to her as she had in London, sometimes an extract from a novel, at others poetry, which her mother loved. And if Elizabeth dozed, as she occasionally did, Becca was happy to sit in quiet contemplation, reliving every moment she had spent with Hugo and wondering what progress he was making across the water.

She had told her mother of her betrothal while they were still in town, for it was inconceivable that Brew would not confide in Harriet at the first opportunity. Thus she was able to speak quite openly with both, and this aided her. "I miss him dreadfully, Harriet, but at least I no longer feel obliged to put him out of my mind, and it is a comfort to be able to talk to you about him." Hugo was her constant companion, in her mind if not in person, and because Harriet and Brew knew him so well, they were happy to talk of him with her.

Her sister-in-law had resumed her habit of riding every day, and Rebecca joined her frequently. Sometimes her brother was busy with other matters, but more often he accompanied them. Becca was delighted also when he offered to teach her to drive, an opportunity that had not previously come her way in those days when Austerly had fallen into a state of disrepair and her father hadn't had time to take an interest in the world about him. It was the praise from Harriet that pleased her most of all, though. "You have light hands, something that was evident when I watched you ride, but you have carried this through to your driving. I have no fear you will damage my horses' mouths."

This was a compliment indeed, for Harriet was accomplished beyond the usual and her horses were her passion.

Between riding, driving and visiting Winthrop to see her niece, who was still at that delightful age where she remained in one place but could gurgle and interact with her admirers, time certainly didn't hang heavy upon Rebecca's hands. There were frequent picnics, dinners and the occasional country dance where she could be assured of seeing Amabel and Gil. Apart from the odd shower, the weather was kind to them. If she suffered from low spirits now and then, it was hardly surprising.

That all changed when at last she received Hugo's letter. She was with her mother when it was brought to her, and she would have reluctantly put it aside until she was alone. However, Elizabeth had no hesitation in sending her off to her room, where she could read in private, and Rebecca dropped a kiss on her mother's cheek and flew out of the door that led not to her bedchamber but gave access to the garden. She moved round the wishing well and tripped into the shrubbery, where she was as certain as she could be that she would remain undisturbed. Seated on a stone bench in the sunshine, she read the letter once very quickly and then more slowly, so as to take everything in.

There was much. Hugo had persuaded Juliette to visit the château, and now he seemed resigned, though perhaps that was too strong a word, to the liaison between his sister and Auguste. By now, both visits would have taken place. How had Isabelle reacted when returning after so many years? Had

Juliette gone under sufferance or willingly? And what of her beau? Her eyes moved lower down the page and her hand went to her breast when she read *Will I return to England and carry you off as my bride?* Somehow she had overlooked this sentence on her first, hasty read. She bit her lower lip in frustration. She had been suppressing her impatience for weeks now. She folded her letter and went directly to her room to pen her reply.

Dearest Hugo

I have been praying, even while I know you are so occupied, that you might have time to write. While it is apparent you have many hurdles yet to leap, it seems they are not so high as you had first supposed, or that you have come to terms with a difficult situation. I hope your meeting with Auguste went well (for you will of course have seen him by the time this reaches you) but I am longing to hear how your mother is, for I only had a brief idea of her feelings as she entered your home.

Here she paused, for there was a question she was burning to ask, but how to phrase it? Directly, she decided, would be the best approach.

Have you yet told her of our engagement? I had not previously considered that upon our marriage, your mother would presumably be expected to retire to whatever equates with a dower house in this country? Is this also the custom in France? That would be cruel indeed, in my opinion. To return home after so many years only to have it snatched away. No, it shall not be. I can only pray that she and I are compatible, and I see no reason why that should not be the case.

There is little to report from Lincolnshire, other than that I am being well cared for and that your goddaughter grows more delightful every time I see her, which is often. It seems impossible that I should see something of my own little Nancy in one so young, but so it is. What a joy for Brew if his daughter should grow to be like our sister.

I shall look forward eagerly to your next letter, when I hope you have much more to tell me. I miss you more than I can say.

Rebecca

In France, things were progressing well. Hugo and Auguste liked each other on sight, and in his presence Hugo noticed a softening in Juliette's features that he hadn't observed before. The bond between them was clear to see, as was the size and elegance of the farmhouse. It was not, as Hugo had imagined, a simple rustic dwelling but a substantial residence around and beyond which were several outbuildings. It had two floors only, but these were spread sufficiently wide and deep as to accommodate any number of rooms. It could have passed for a nobleman's home and was perhaps as great a lesson as any Hugo had ever learned in not making assumptions.

"You are surprised? I can tell," Auguste said, shaking his hand. His smile was one of the highest amusement. It was returned.

"What can I say, Auguste? I have been put in my place, that much is certain."

"Do not scorn those of a different class, *mon ami*. There are several working on my property without whom I could not run the farm efficiently and to whom I have much cause to be grateful."

"Wait till you meet Henri. No-one is better than he at reprimanding me when I get above myself. He is my valet and I would be lost without him, and not because he takes such good care of my clothes."

"You understand, then."

"Unquestionably."

Isabelle and Juliette were both becoming impatient at their exclusion from the conversation, and the latter interrupted indignantly, "Perhaps you might show my brother some of the rooms so he may see where I —" she paused — "and Maman will be residing."

Hugo knew better than to respond to this deliberate provocation, but he was liking his sister more and more each time they met. No meek and mild creature was she. Becoming better acquainted would be interesting. All things considered, marriage to a gentleman farmer would suit her admirably and, far from being averse to the connection, Hugo found himself to be delighted and more than a little relieved.

But what of their mother? Was Juliette in the right? Would living with her daughter for a while be a better solution than returning to an environment from which she had been absent half her life, and which she would have to share with a young woman with whom she was unacquainted? It must be for Isabelle to decide.

Thoughts of Rebecca made him long to return to her side. If his sister's nuptials were to proceed swiftly, he would remain in France until then. Not waiting until things were resolved but anxious to have some contact with his betrothed, even if only by means of the post, he wrote again.

My dearest darling

Needless to say how much I am missing you, but I will say it nonetheless. When I left you, I left a part of me behind.

Things are progressing far better than I might have anticipated, and I hope to return to England more speedily than I had previously thought possible. I must wait a while, though, until after my sister's wedding. Yes, that is to go ahead. I am filled with remorse for my earlier response. Auguste is a charming man, a gentleman farmer, not the yokel I had imagined. And in any case, who am I to judge a man's character by his social status? I am ashamed and hope I have learned my lesson well.

Maman and Juliette were delighted when I told them of our own betrothal and cannot wait to meet you.

He lifted the pen from the page and took the end between his teeth, and a smile of pure amusement lit up his eyes. Perhaps he was overstating the case. Of course they were gratified he had found happiness, so he wasn't fibbing exactly.

You asked about my mother's reaction when she came to the château. Rebecca, she was like an excited child, running from room to room. Her mood changed instantly, though, once we entered the secret chamber, and there was a chill that had nothing to do with the temperature. We closed the door, and she expressed her intention never to go there again but, my darling, I wish you could have seen her when I took her then to the library and placed her jewellery box before her.

The visit ended well, and I met Auguste the following day. I couldn't be happier at the way things are proceeding and hope you may look for me before too long. In the meantime, my dearest, tread gently, for you carry my heart.

Hugo

CHAPTER EIGHTEEN

Rebecca, in spite of all her good intentions, was becoming restless. It had been a while since she'd received Hugo's last letter, and with nothing to guide her she could only speculate as to what might be happening across the water. In anticipation of her proposed new role in life, she'd been working hard on improving her French and in this she was aided by Amabel Carstairs. Gil's wife was proficient — or at least more so than Becca — because as a child, while her sister Harriet had spent every moment she could in the stables, Amabel had been a diligent student. Somehow, the conversations between the two young women — conducted exclusively in that language and the cause of much amusement as one or other struggled for a word or phrase to fit the circumstances — contrived to make Rebecca feel closer to Hugo. In her solitary moments, though, she couldn't help wondering if she would receive another letter or if her flamboyant fiancé might arrive one day out of the blue.

Notwithstanding, it wasn't Hugo who travelled to Austerly but his valet, Henri, and it was immediately obvious that all was not well. Upon his demanding to be shown immediately to Miss Ware, the footman had had no hesitation in taking him directly to the drawing room in spite of him being unshaven, dishevelled and ashen-faced. It needed no great intellect to discern that he carried bad tidings. It happened that Harriet and Brew were visiting on the afternoon he arrived, a happy chance in the light of the dreadful news that Henri brought with him.

"Major Ware," he began, judging it best to address him, but he was looking at Rebecca, "I have come from the coast. There has been a terrible accident. We had almost reached harbour when some freak weather occurred. Our boat was tossed about as though it were no more than a cork, and then it broke up." He stopped to gulp in some air, so distressed was he.

Rebecca, as pale as the lace on her gown, was standing rigid, having risen as soon as Henri had entered the room. She said nothing, though her hand rose to her throat.

"I was thrown onto a beach not far from what had been our destination. People came to help. I was half drowned, you understand, and when I came fully to my senses it took me a full day to recover."

Henri paused again and Brew, who had moved to his sister's side, said, "Go on, man. What happened next?"

Henri could not continue. He broke down in tears and the major, who knew him well, waited patiently for what he anticipated was to come, only telling him to sit down before he should fall.

"I searched for three days. I found two others, who told me they had clung to some wreckage before being picked up, but of my master there was no sign. I visited inns. I knocked on doors. *Rien.* There was no sign of him, Mademoiselle," he finished, this time looking directly at Rebecca, his voice breaking on a sob.

Her unnatural rigidity crumbled and, despite her brother's supporting hand, she fell to the floor in a dead faint. Brew picked her up and carried her to the sofa, at the same time shouting for the footman to fetch her abigail, the devoted Alice. So shallow was the rise and fall of her breast that for a moment he feared she had expired from shock. As Alice entered, he moved aside.

"Your mistress has received some bad news. It would help her, I think, if you could loosen her stays. I know nothing of such things," Brew said. He turned his attention to Henri, who by now had brought himself under control and was staring bleakly at nothing in particular. As Brew approached him, he made to stand.

"No, man, stay where you are. You must be exhausted. There can be no doubt, I suppose?"

"I did everything I could, Major."

"Of course. I hope I need not assure you that you may stay with my family at Winthrop."

Henri looked at him straight. "I'd appreciate that, sir, for a few days if I may, but then I must return to France. His mother, you understand. And his sister. They do not know."

Brew's expression was grim indeed. What pitiless fate had brought this family together after so many years, only to tear them apart so cruelly? He called the footman again, asking that he take the broken man to a room where he might rest for a while and regain some strength. Probably overnight, for there was no doubt he was exhausted. Tomorrow he would fetch him and take him to Winthrop, but in the meantime he would tell Harriet what had passed. He had a plan that he was certain his wife would agree to, but that he was equally sure she would not like.

Rebecca was beginning to stir, so he returned to her side to give what comfort he could. She opened her eyes and they flickered from one thing to another, as though she did not know where she was. The familiar surroundings did much to help and she finally brought her gaze to her brother, kneeling helplessly by her side and stroking her hands.

"Brew! I see from your face that I am not waking from a bad dream but to a living nightmare. My poor Hugo. What a horrible way to die."

His admiration and respect for his sister knew no bounds at that moment. Her thoughts were not for herself and her loss, as might have been expected, but for Hugo and his suffering. It seemed the Wares had learned over the years to deal with such grievous happenings. She asked to be taken to her mother and they went together to the drawing room at the back of the house, Elizabeth's personal domain. There they told her what had happened. She too presented a stoic front, but all three turned to the window to look upon the wishing well, where that first tragedy had occurred so many years ago.

Becca at last dropped into a short-lived sleep in the early hours of the morning, but even her dreams were filled with terrifying images of mountainous waves and shipwrecks. She was grateful when her maid brought her some hot chocolate, but as she sat in bed trying to think of what she might do next the tears finally fell, followed by gulping sobs that left a pain in her chest and an ache in her heart that she feared would never heal. Nothing in her short and often tragic life had prepared her for this blow which had left in its wake a feeling of such helplessness as she had never known before.

How shall I go on without you, my darling? It was a question she asked often in the coming hours and days, but go on she must. Her parents had already lost one daughter. They had been estranged from their son for more years than any of them cared to remember and, even though reconciliation had come, the memories had not passed. For their sakes alone, she wouldn't follow her instinct to throw herself from the tallest window. Her salvation, or at least the manner of moving forward, came from her brother. He'd returned to Austerly on the day following Henri's arrival to carry him back to Winthrop. It was then that he'd repeated to Becca much of his conversation with his wife.

"Harriet will come over later to express her condolences in person."

Becca knew that before meeting Brew, her sister-in-law had suffered a similar loss when her then fiancé had been slain at the Battle of Waterloo. She would understand better than any the grief she was suffering.

"That is kind of her indeed."

"No such thing. But I would tell you what passed between us when I arrived home. You may imagine her shock, and I had difficulty holding her back from coming to see you immediately. I then went on to tell her what I plan to do next. You may not have heard Henri expressing his intention to return to France as soon as he is fit. To inform Isabelle and Juliette, you understand. Well, it is my intention to travel with him. He and Hugo were so much closer than master and man."

He paused as his sister waved her hand helplessly, as if to ward off yet another blow.

"I feel obliged to do what I can for him, as well as the family. I am to travel with him, for it is not a task he should undertake alone. Harriet agrees, though I will of necessity be gone for some time." He didn't tell Rebecca how she had clung to him, understanding his motives yet dreading their parting.

"I will come with you," Becca declared.

"What! Don't be a fool, Becca. What good will it do you?"

"I know from Hugo's last letter that he had informed Isabelle and Juliette of our betrothal. It cannot be thought an intrusion, then, if I join you. I will be able to tell them things about him they do not know, and the same may happen in reverse. It is possible we may all draw some comfort from such a meeting. You must allow me this, Brew. I beg you."

It wasn't the clutching of his sleeve that persuaded him but the clarity of her intent and the possibility that some degree of solace might be experienced by all.

"I had planned to ride." Even as he spoke, he knew it was a futile gesture.

"Then you may be my escort."

"Becca…"

"My mind is made up, Brew. Please say you will take me with you."

"I would give Henri another full day to recover. Prepare to travel the day after tomorrow. For now, he and I will return to Winthrop. I shall leave it to you to tell our parents of our plans."

Harriet rode over later in the day. Not much was said about Hugo, for there wasn't much they could say. They walked in the gardens, mostly in silence, sometimes talking about young Nancy. When the time came to part, the two women embraced and as Harriet rode off, she looked back over her shoulder to see Rebecca waving to her. There was a bond between them that gave comfort to the forlorn young woman standing alone. But she had a purpose now, and that would carry her through the next period. What might come after that, she wasn't prepared to think about.

Elizabeth and Cornelius didn't put up much of a fight. They would have preferred Rebecca to remain at home where they might give whatever comfort they were able, but they had learned to accept the wilfulness of their children. It was, after all, part of their strength. With Brew urging them to visit Harriet and their granddaughter often in his absence, they would be occupied enough. Elizabeth waved from the steps as her husband shook their son's hand. At least the family feud had been resolved.

In the carriage, Rebecca and her maid maintained silence, gazing out of the window. Thoughts of what might be to come occupied Rebecca's mind and helped her to focus on something other than her loss. Brew found a coaching inn large enough to accommodate all four, without the need for Alice to sleep on a truckle bed in Rebecca's chamber, and he hired a private room besides so they could dine in comfort, just the two of them, while Alice and Henri were taken care of elsewhere. Brew had left his own valet, François, at Winthrop, much to his disgust.

"But, monsieur, you will surely not travel without me," he had protested, his indignation palpable and the more so because another would be taking his place.

"You are being ridiculous. What possible need could I have of two valets on such a journey? Henri will serve me well, you may be sure."

"But what if he remains in France when you return?"

Brew raised an eyebrow. It spoke more than any words. "The coat with the silver buttons, if you please. You will not wish to delay me when my wife is waiting to dine."

No more had been said. The major, François knew, was — like any soldier — perfectly capable of looking after himself for a few days, but he would have given much to have gone with him.

After they had crossed the Channel, Rebecca became quieter as the prospect of what was to happen came more to the fore. She was to be the bringer of terrible news. How could she expect to form a relationship with a woman whom she would be plunging into despair? Her own grief had rendered her uncommunicative. Would Isabelle turn her back? Had she been wrong in insisting that Brew take her with him? Too late now, but the length of the days in the carriage gave her much cause for reflection. The magic of the scenery was lost upon her as her thoughts turned inwards.

Finally they arrived at the Château du Berge on a beautiful sunlit afternoon. Becca gasped at the imposing structure and at any other time would have delighted in its quaint turrets, looking more like something out of a fairy tale than a place where real people lived. Even the twinkling of the sun on the water of the Loire, visible below them, added an enchantment. Brew grasped her trembling fingers as he aided her down from the coach, and together they approached the entrance. The major, his French fluent by reason of having lived in the country for several years, explained to the footman that they desired to see the comtesse.

"She is in the garden, monsieur. I will take you to her."

A woman, small of stature and with raven hair, was cutting a rose and laying it in her basket along with others. She looked up at their approach, a smile and a question displayed on her features. Becca's steps faltered, for there could be no doubt of the connection.

"*Bonjour. Puis-je vous aider?*"

It was Brew who carried the conversation. He broke the news, for although Becca had worked diligently at the language she was not sufficiently proficient to converse when so overcome by her emotions. She was able to follow, though. At first he introduced himself and his sister. Under such circumstances, Isabelle, no fool, could not but know something was wrong. Her son had gone to fetch his bride and she had arrived without him. She sank onto a stone bench and the basket of flowers slipped from her fingers, the contents breaking on the ground.

This woman had suffered so much loss in her life but this, when she had thought at last all was well, rendered her incapable of speech or action. She only wept silently, while they waited. Eventually, she said, "It was too good to be true. I should have known that fate would not deal kindly with me."

When they explained the circumstances she wept some more, grieving that there would be no grave in which to lay Hugo to rest.

"I must tell Juliette. It is too late now to go to Sully-sur-Loire. In any case, I am in no haste to carry such dreadful news. Come inside. The château is sufficiently restored that most of the rooms are now habitable. I will arrange accommodation for you." But as they returned to the entrance hall, they found Alice and Henri still waiting. When she saw him she broke down once more, and he with her.

"Madame, I would have given my life for him. You know that," he assured her.

Some few hours later Isabelle sat down to dine with her guests, though not one of the three had any appetite. Rebecca was seated on her left, and she laid her hand upon the one that rested on the table. With a deep sigh, she said, "This is not how I anticipated welcoming you home, my child. Hugo was so excited and, I know, at the same time anxious that we should get along. I wish I could tell him that his apprehension was unfounded. I was prepared to love you for his sake. Now I am ready to love you for your own. Tomorrow you will meet my daughter, and I hope you will extend your stay, for I should be glad of your company. You must have much to tell me about my son. I am eager to hear everything, every snippet of conversation you can remember, the places you visited together. Your memories will become my memories, for I have nothing else."

Juliette was more greatly distressed than Rebecca had anticipated. It seemed that in the short time they'd known each other, and after their shaky start, Hugo and his sister had become close. Their loss brought all three women together, and Auguste tactfully drew Brew to one side to allow them to commiserate together.

"Permit me, if you will, to show you something of the estate while you are here." He smiled, remembering Hugo's reaction. "My brother-in-law was surprised when first he came here, imagining I was asking his sister to live with me in a peasant's hut." He looked across at the women, who were in close conversation. "I think we may allow ourselves some time, don't you?"

Brew was delighted to oblige. It hadn't been so very long since the management of Austerly had been placed in his hands, and he was very aware that he still had much to learn. Auguste's land was extensive and in far better order than his own, but that would come, he was determined. There was much information he could acquire from the Frenchman, and the day was consequently considerably advanced when they returned to the farmhouse. By this time, Becca, Isabelle and Juliette had come to an understanding, and a decision had been made.

"It has been decided that I will remain with Isabelle at the château for the time being, a day or two not being sufficient for us to say everything that needs to be said. Harriet will be anxious, our parents also. Pray tell them … well, you will know what to say."

Brew made no attempt to change her mind. It would have been futile, he knew, and he judged also that if ever Rebecca's broken heart was to heal, it would do so more easily in this environment. Two days later he left for home, charging Henri with the task of accompanying his sister when she chose to return to England.

CHAPTER NINETEEN

Henri did much to aid the three women in the coming days. He had spent more time with Hugo than any of them, and far more as a friend than as his valet. He entertained them with stories of their time together, being careful to omit such details as were unsuitable for tender ears. He made them laugh and he made them cry, but he brought Hugo closer than anyone else could have done. In between all this, he had to liaise with the steward regarding the completion of renovations and decorations, such that Isabelle was moved to say, "You have made yourself as indispensable to me as you did to my son. You have intimated that you have no family ties. I beg you will remain at the château, for a place like this needs a man at the helm."

Rebecca showed no disposition to return to England. Not only did she feel closer to Hugo in France, but a bond had formed between her and Isabelle such as she had never known with any woman other than her mother. Three weeks after Brew had left them, they were in the rose garden, cutting the last of the blooms when Becca looked up and was confronted by a ghost.

"Hugo! HUGO!"

She raced to the gap in the wall where he had appeared and threw herself onto his chest. He caught her and held her in his arms, managing to prevent them both from falling by grasping a frame which served to accommodate a climbing bush.

"*Doucement, ma chérie*, I am not yet fully recovered."

He looked over her shoulder at his mother, rooted to the spot, unable to believe the evidence of her eyes.

"*Oui*, Maman, you are not deceived."

He led Rebecca to where Isabelle was standing and all three sat on a bench. Becca gripped his hand, demanding, "How can this be? It has been weeks."

"How much do you know?"

"Henri came straight to Austerly, a broken man for he could find no trace of you. You would not believe how hard he searched, how many doors he knocked upon in case you had been taken in."

"My poor Henri. You relieve my mind, for my greatest worry has been that he did not survive the wreck. His instinct was right. I was indeed taken up for dead, but the Comte du Berge does not give in so easily. I was not entirely unconscious but delirious, and apparently in my crazed state I gabbled away in French. As a consequence, I was taken not to England but to France and left in the care of a fisherman and his wife."

"A blessing on her. I can understand that you needed time to recover, my dearest, but why did you not send word?"

Hugo laughed. Both women thought they had never heard a sweeter sound.

"For a while I was out of my mind. *Et puis*, when that passed I had no recollection of the accident, of who I was and where I had come from, or indeed where I was going. All my possessions had gone down with the ship and I was wearing nothing that might identify me except for my signet ring, but it is merely a gold band with a stone. No markings. No insignia. It was obviously valuable and told me something of my status — unless I had been a thief and stolen it — but there was nothing that might determine who I was."

"You must have been terrified!" Rebecca exclaimed.

"How astute of you," he said, dropping a kiss on the top of her head, which was resting on his shoulder. "I have never been so frightened in my whole life, not even the time when I would have died had Henri not rescued me from my assailants many years ago. Where is he, by the way? Did he remain in England? And how do you come to be here, my darling?"

"Brew and Henri brought me here, for someone had to tell your mother and Juliette what had happened. What we thought had happened," she corrected herself. "My brother has returned home, but Henri remains."

"Then I must find him immediately and put his mind at rest."

But when he tried to stand he stumbled, and it was clear he was not entirely recovered.

"Wait here with Isabelle, and I will bring him to you. I believe he is in the west tower and will not have observed your arrival. How did you come here?"

"I rode."

"Wait here, then. I shall not be long."

She was reluctant to leave him, but the knowledge that he was safe with Isabelle and that Henri needed to hear the news spurred her on. Some mischief prevented her from telling him what had occurred, just that his presence was required in the rose garden. For a second time he broke down in tears, but these were tears of joy and as the two men embraced she felt her world turn back to rights.

It was then that Hugo finished his tale. During his time with the fisherman and his wife, it had become evident that Hugo was as fluent in English as he was in French, and this was even more perplexing for he could have come from either side of the Channel. He began to regain his physical strength, but any details of his history remained hidden from him. Then, after a couple of weeks, he began to have flashbacks. "Nothing coherent, you understand, but your face appeared to me many times, Rebecca. I saw a château. This one, obviously, though I knew it not at the time. Once I pictured myself riding into a village and stopping outside a peasant's cottage. Sully-sur-Loire, I assume. You must understand, everything was very hazy. One thing became clear. Most visions I had were of places in France. The architecture is quite different and there could be no mistaking it. Then names came back to me. Yours, Rebecca, and yours, Maman, and also Juliette's and Henri's. Even Brew's. I remember being puzzled, for what sort of name is that? I didn't recall at the time that it was formed using the first letters of each of his names: Benedict Richmond Edward Ware. Then a scene appeared to me of the two of us, Becca, and we were holding a child. Was I married, perhaps?"

Rebecca blushed. "No, but it is my dearest wish that you soon will be."

It had been a vision of when they were at Merivale, of course, just before he had left for France that first time in search of his sister.

"We must tell Juliette," Isabelle said.

"I will go," said Henri.

"*Non. S'il vous plaît.* I will go myself," said Hugo.

"But not today, my boy. What she doesn't yet know will not harm her. You must rest now, for it is evident you are exhausted. You can tell us more later. For the time being, it is sufficient you are here."

Hugo attempted to protest, but three people whose prime concern was his welfare were having none of it. He allowed himself to be escorted inside, and Henri took him to his bedchamber from where nothing more was heard of him for some hours. Rebecca and Isabelle were at a loss as to what to do with themselves in the meantime. The joy of having him back left them elated, but each needed an outlet for their newly found energy. Hugo's mother found hers in gathering some foliage and arranging the flowers they had picked earlier. Rebecca sat in the same room and occupied herself with writing a letter to Brew. The sooner he learned the good news, the better.

My darling brother,

You will not believe what has happened. Hugo is alive! Somehow he survived and was picked up and brought to France. I don't know all the details yet, for he only arrived a short while ago and is now sleeping. He was badly knocked up and is not fully recovered. I believe there is no lasting damage. I pray that is the case. What I have ascertained is that he suffered from memory loss and his rescuers had no idea as to his identity. That is the reason we did not hear from him. You may imagine our reaction when we saw him. We were in the garden and he just appeared like a ghost risen from the dead, but he is real enough, my dearest. Tomorrow, if he is strong enough, he will ride to Sully-sur-Loire. Henri will go with him in case he is needed.

Everything is now up in the air, of course. I don't know what will happen next, but it is fairly certain I will not return to Austerly any time soon. I will not come without Hugo, and I don't know how long it will be before he is fit enough or would even wish to undertake the journey. I will write to our mother also when I know more, but I felt it imperative to send you this news, so good as it is.

My love to Harriet and Nancy, big brother, and, well, I don't know what else to say other than I did not believe I would ever be happy again, and now...

Becca

She laid her pen down just as Isabelle finished her own task. Instead of returning to his work in the west wing, Henri had taken up position in Hugo's dressing room, ready to attend to him when he awoke. He'd promised to seek them out when his master came downstairs, so they went for a walk down to the river, leaving word as to where they'd gone. Both needed some physical activity to prevent them pacing up and down. It was two hours later, as they were returning to the château, that Henri came to meet them.

"Hugo is well rested and would have come in search of you himself, had I not prevented him from doing so."

Rebecca frowned. "He must be weak indeed if he would allow you to overrule him so easily."

Henri laughed. "Did I say it was easy?"

She was satisfied only when she entered the room and Hugo leaped to his feet and crushed her in his arms.

"Forgive me, Maman, but I could not help myself," he said, smiling at Isabelle over the top of Becca's head.

His mother was indulgent but demanded an embrace of her own. "Only then will I be sure you have returned to us."

"Be assured I am real enough. Tomorrow I will go to Juliette. We have fixed it between us, Henri and I, that we will take the carriage so you need not worry that I am taxing my strength."

The valet had done his work well. He and Isabelle withdrew, albeit a little reluctantly, to leave Rebecca and Hugo alone. For a while they sat in silence, content merely to be together again. Finally, she raised her head from where it rested upon his shoulder and said in a very small voice, "You came back here, not to England." It was a statement, but there was no doubting the question.

A finger imperatively raised her chin. "Because I was not fit to travel. Do you not know I would have given anything to rush to your side? Foolish girl. My life is bound up in yours. Without you, it is not worth living." And then he proved it by pressing his lips against hers and crushing her in his arms. She was content.

Now that he was back, Hugo's recovery proceeded at a greater rate than they might have hoped for. Inevitably came discussions about their forthcoming nuptials, and he had to raise his concerns.

"I am worried about your position here at the château. I had thought that after we were wed, Maman might choose to live with Juliette and Auguste, but she seems to show no disposition to do so."

"Oh no, and you must not ask it of her. She has treated me as a daughter ever since I arrived, even before we knew you were safe. We lived together for several weeks in perfect harmony, and I see no reason why that should not continue. Do you have any objection to such an arrangement?"

"Not I. But you? You do not object?"

"Of course not. In a while, I would like to pay an extended visit to England, maybe for a month or two, and perhaps your mother could come with us if she desires. It may be that she would wish to visit your house there, to see the home in which you were raised by Pierre."

Hugo showed his approval in the usual way and, only a little flustered, Becca continued, "After that, I make no doubt that when we return to France, Isabelle and I will live together amicably." She looked at him from under her lashes, her expression so coy that he was moved once more to gather her into his arms.

"I cannot wait to call you mine."

"Nor I, Hugo. It is but a few days now until the wedding."

They were married quietly in the local church, and Isabelle went to stay in Sully-sur-Loire for a few days while they remained at the château. A few weeks later, Rebecca received a letter from her brother.

My dearest Becca,

All is well here and we look forward to welcoming you whenever you and your husband are ready to travel. You may wish to know that Harriet's sister is with child and that your young friend Emily Waddesdon, whom you tried so hard to help, was last week wed to Robert Saltaire. No doubt you will be delighted at such an outcome.

I must congratulate you again on your own situation. It would seem after all that you were right about your prince.

There was more but she showed this page to her husband, knowing that after his part in the affair, he would be pleased for Emily. He was indeed, but his eye dropped lower and he asked, "What is all this about a prince?"

Becca laughed and told him it was an old family joke, for she had once told Brew she would find a prince to marry. Hugo may have been only a comte in name, but to Rebecca he would always be her prince.

A NOTE TO THE READER

Dear Reader

I hope you have enjoyed reading *Some Day My Prince Will Come* as much as I enjoyed writing it. If you would consider leaving a review on **Amazon** or **Goodreads**, it would be much appreciated, though I would be just as happy if you'd like to join me on my **Facebook author page** for a chat. You can also visit me on **Twitter**, **Instagram** and my **website**.

Natalie

nataliekleinman.com

Sapere Books is an exciting new publisher of brilliant fiction and popular history.

To find out more about our latest releases and our monthly bargain books visit our website:
saperebooks.com

Printed in Great Britain
by Amazon

26398348R10126